Three Girl Chums at Laurel Hall

Or The Mystery of the School by the Lake

May Hollis Barton

Three Girl Chums at Laurel Hall or The Mystery of the School by the Lake

The present edition is a reproduction of previous publication of this classic work. Minor typographical errors may have been corrected without note; however, for an authentic reading experience the spelling, punctuation, and capitalization have been retained from the original text.

ISBN: 979-8-89773-040-7

CONTENTS

CHAPTER I

JO'S TROUBLE

"Jo! You never mean it!"

Nan Harrison regarded the dark-haired girl with dismay.

"I'm afraid I do," said Jo Morley miserably. "You don't hate it any more than I do, Nan!"

"You said you couldn't go with us to Laurel Hall," said the third of the trio, repeating the statement made by Jo Morley a moment before as though she still could not credit it. "Why, Jo, it was only yesterday we were talking over our plans for boarding school! You expected to go then, didn't you?"

"Of course I did! I learned the awful news only last night!"

Over Jo's dark head Nan Harrison and Sadie Appleby exchanged frowning glances. Then Nan slipped a coaxing arm within Jo's.

"Suppose you tell us all about it, Jo," she said. "It's the worst news in the world, of course, but we might as well hear it now as later."

"I hardly understand about it myself, yet," said poor Jo, with a telltale quiver of her lips. "But it has something to do with Dad's business. He's had a heavy money loss, as he calls it, and—and he can't afford to send me away to boarding school. That's all."

"All!" echoed Nan Harrison, aghast. "It's enough! Why, Jo, if you can't go to Laurel Hall it will just spoil everything! I don't want to go at all!"

"Nor I!" said Sadie Appleby.

The three girls walked along moodily for a distance, pondering this unexpected change in their prospects.

Nan Harrison, the tallest of the three chums, was fair-haired and blue-eyed, a fine specimen of the athletic schoolgirl. Jo

Morley formed a rather striking contrast to Nan in that her hair and eyes were as dark as Nan's were fair. Jo was small, too, and as lithe and active on her feet as a little cat.

Sadie Appleby, on the other hand, was rather a cross between the two, being of medium height, and having light brown hair and gray eyes.

The three girls had been chums all through the years of grammar school. It was their boast that nothing and nobody could separate them, that where one went the other two were sure to follow.

The happy association of grammar school days at an end, they had planned to go together to famous Laurel Hall boarding school which was situated about two hundred miles west of their home town of Woodford.

Their names had been entered with Miss Jane Romaine, the presiding head of Laurel Hall, a year before the delightful, late-summer day on which poor Jo was breaking her news to her dismayed chums. It was a well known fact that there was always a waiting list of those who aspired to enter the select portals of Laurel Hall, and that not all who applied were admitted.

So there was great rejoicing on the part of the three girls when their parents had received word from Miss Romaine that their applications had been accepted and that the girls' names had been enrolled among those who would enter the following fall.

It would be such great fun! The three chums had looked forward to it as such a marvelous experience! And now all their happy plans must be overshadowed by this inexplicable statement of Jo's in regard to her father's business!

"Maybe your father didn't mean it," said Sadie, a desperate gleam of hope in her eye. "Maybe he was just fooling you."

Jo shook her head gravely.

"That isn't Dad's idea of a joke, Sadie," she said. "If you could have seen him when he told me," she added, with a miserable little shake of the head, "you wouldn't think he was joking!"

"Is it very bad, Jo?" Nan bent down and tried to peer into her chum's downcast face. "Your father was always well off. Surely, he can't have lost every cent of his money at once!"

Again Jo shook her head, frowning.

"I tell you, I don't understand about it altogether, Nan," she answered. "Dad was so blue last night that I didn't like to question him much."

"How did he come to tell you about it?" Sadie insisted.

The shadow of trouble deepened on Jo's face, and for a moment she walked on between the two girls in silence, her eyes on the ground.

"It was last night after dinner," she said finally, speaking rapidly as though she did not like to remember the scene she was about to describe. "I was raving on about Laurel Hall and wishing the last days of vacation would fly a little faster so that we could start in there when Dad turned around and looked at me. There was—there was a look on his face that frightened me!"

For a time Sadie and Nan said nothing; just stared at Jo with a tragic expression.

"Well—" prompted Nan at last.

"Well," Jo sighed, "he told me I'd better not count too much on going to Laurel Hall. At first I thought it must be a joke, but when I saw Mother over in a corner crying into one of Dad's pocket handkerchiefs, I saw it was all true enough."

"But what did he say?" persisted Sadie, who was always insatiable for details.

"Just what I told you before. That he had been unfortunate in business and had lost a great deal of money, and that he couldn't afford to send me away to school. Poor old Dad, he took it pretty hard, too. So did Mother. I wish there was something I could do to help."

"Same here!" said Nan unhappily. "This is awful, Jo!"

"It's positive cruelty to animals," agreed Sadie. "I think I'll sit right down when I get home and write out a resignation to Miss Jane Romaine. I shan't stir a step if you don't, Jo, and that settles it!"

"I'm not a dog in the manger," said Jo, with a mirthless smile. "It won't help me any to have your good time spoiled."

"Our good time!" cried Nan. "As if it wasn't spoiled already if you can't go with us! I can't believe the awful truth yet. I simply can't!"

The three girls had been for a hike out into the country. Now they realized suddenly that it was getting late, and they turned their steps toward home.

They walked on for a considerable distance in silence, each busy with her own thoughts. Suddenly Nan spoke.

"We've got troubles at home, too, though of course they are nothing like yours, Jo," she said. "Dad has money enough yet, thank goodness! But poor Aunt Emma—" she paused and a shadow clouded her face.

Jo and Sadie knew of Nan's Aunt Emma, although they had seen very little of the maiden lady who lived with the Harrisons. The latter was half-paralyzed, an all but helpless invalid. Week after week, month after month, she sat in her wheeled chair near the window of her room, reading, sewing, or sitting idle, hands clasped in her lap looking out upon a scene of which she could never again hope to be an active part. So now when Nan spoke the invalid's name Jo and Sadie were all sympathy.

"Why, what's the matter with your Aunt Emma—worse than usual, I mean?" asked Jo.

"You look so dreadfully sad, Nan," added Sadie.

Nan shook her head.

"It's enough to make any one sad, to see that poor patient woman sitting there week after week and year after year, watching other people do what she is crazy to do herself. But that isn't the worst. Lately, it seems to us," Nan paused and stared at the girls tragically, "as if poor Aunt Emma were losing her mind!"

The girls cried out, shocked:

"Oh, Nan, you never mean that!"

"The few times I have spoken to her she seemed unusually quick-witted," protested Jo.

Nan nodded.

"She doesn't talk much any more, though, and when she does she says—funny things. Too much brooding, Dad says. He believes that if something would only happen to shock her out of this state of mind and give her a new interest in life, she might have a chance. As it is, we are all dreadfully worried about her."

They had been walking slowly toward town.

"If we want to get home in time for dinner," Sadie observed, "I guess we'll just about have to run!"

They did run, but on reaching the outskirts of the town they slowed their progress to a quick but decorous walk. They had not gone more than two or three blocks, however, when Jo stopped and sniffed the air in a curious manner.

"What's wrong with you?" Sadie wanted to know. "You look like a pointer dog."

"Thanks for the comparison," retorted Jo. "Does anybody smell smoke?"

"Yes! And I see it, too!" Nan pointed toward a cloud of smoke that curled lazily skyward. "It looks as though it came from my street! Girls, it can't be our house!"

The girls turned the corner of the street and found that their worst fears were justified. Smoke was rolling in gray clouds from the windows of the Harrison house!

"It seems to be downstairs!" gasped Nan.

The girls ran swiftly toward the house, but as they reached it a sound came to them that chilled their blood. They stared at each other, white-faced, desperate. For that sound had been a cry for help!

Nan pointed to an upper window.

"Aunt Emma's room!" she cried. "The fire has reached her room! She will die like a rat in a trap! Girls, we've got to get her out! We've got to!"

Again from the room above came that fearful, heartbreaking cry.

"Help! Oh, help!"

CHAPTER II

FIRE!

The three girls dashed to the front door of the Harrison house but were met and driven back by a cloud of smoke.

"The dining room's full of it!" cried Nan. "Probably the stairs are afire!"

"We'll have to reach the room from the outside," declared Jo.

Ever the leader in moments when level head and quick action were needed, Jo Morley looked about her.

Painters had been at work on the outside of the house. These had finished their day's work, but had left behind them some paint cans, an empty bucket or two, and a long ladder.

The three girls saw it at the same instant, but Jo was the first to reach it.

Together they raised the heavy ladder and with much straining effort brought it around to the rear of the house.

The cries of the invalid could still be heard, but they were becoming terrifyingly faint and weak.

"Oh, hurry, hurry!" almost sobbed Nan. "If we don't reach her soon it will be too late— —"

"You two stay here and hold the ladder!" Jo commanded briskly. "I'm going up!"

"No, Jo! Let me go!" cried Nan.

But Jo Morley was already half way up the ladder, scaling it like a monkey.

Fortunately, a shed stretched beneath one window of the invalid's room. This shed had been added to the house after construction, and was used by the Harrisons as a pantry. The roof of the shed, Jo noticed swiftly, was almost level.

"There's luck, anyway!" she thought, as she hopped nimbly from the ladder to the shed roof and ran over toward the open window.

A cloud of smoke rolled from this aperture, suffocating smoke that caught in Jo's throat and choked her. She turned aside for a moment, drew in a long breath of clean, cool air, then plunged bravely through the window into the room beyond.

The smoke stung her eyes. Blinded, Jo groped with feverish hands.

"Miss Emma!" she cried. "Where are you? Help me to find you!"

"Here I am—right here!"

The voice, though faint, was close to her. Jo turned sharply and stumbled over a chair. Her tortured eyes saw dimly a figure straining toward her.

"Help me out! Help me out! This smoke! I can't fight it any longer!"

Jo's strong young arms went about the slender, wasted figure in the chair.

"If you can put your arm over my shoulders—that's it! Now I'll have you out in a jiffy!"

Jo spoke more confidently than she felt. The smoke swirled about her like a living thing; it robbed her of sight; it sapped her strength. To carry this helpless invalid to the safety of the shed roof seemed at the moment utterly beyond her power.

"I can't do it! I can't do it!" she cried. Then, with a sudden stiffening of her will: "I will do it!"

Even in her torment of mind and body, Jo found time to wonder why there was no flame.

"All smoke and no fire!" she thought.

She wound her arms more tightly about the invalid. A sudden sagging of the woman's weight frightened her. A quick glance confirmed her fear. Aunt Emma had fainted!

Jo summoned all her strength and staggered with her burden toward the square of window. She could not lift the invalid; could only drag her step by step away from the torment of the smoke-filled room.

What if the woman was dead? She was so heavy!

Jo's throat was parched. The blood pounded in her temples. Tears from her tortured eyes ran down her face.

Only a step more— —

She reached the sill. Gasping, she rested her burden on the sill for a moment, striving for breath. A cloud of smoke rolled over her, stifling, blinding.

Suppose Miss Emma were dead! One breath of fresh air— —

Jo tried to lift the unconscious woman across the sill. Useless! Her strength had deserted her. Her head whirled dizzily. Only the grip of her hand on the window sill kept her on her feet.

"Oh, what shall I do! What shall I do?" she cried aloud in her impotence. "Help me, some one! Help me!"

As though in answer to her cry, a figure appeared on the shed outside the window.

"Jo, have you got her?" The voice was Nan's.

Jo cried in an agony of relief:

"Oh, I'm so glad you came, glad! Can you help me get her over the window sill?"

Some one else was on the shed, and Jo knew vaguely that it was Sadie. They had both come to help her. Well, it was just in the nick of time!

Between them, the chums managed to get the unconscious woman over the window sill and on to the shed roof outside. Jo, relieved of her burden, scrambled over herself.

She stood there for a moment breathing in deep breaths of the pure evening air. Then she looked toward the invalid.

The latter was stretched out on the shed, her head pillowed on Nan's arm. Nan was crying over and over again that they had come too late; that her aunt was dead.

Sadie looked on dumbly at the scene, frightened and not knowing just how to help.

Jo pushed her aside and knelt beside the invalid.

"She isn't dead. Look, Nan. She's breathing, and there's color in her face!"

Nan's face brightened and she raised the helpless head that rested on her arm.

"If we could only get her down off this shed!" Sadie Appleby was looking nervously at the black smoke that rolled from the window. "The fire may break out any minute!"

"How are we going to get her down the ladder?" Nan waved her hand helplessly. "Not one of us is strong enough and there's no one else in sight."

She was wrong there. Jo ran to the edge of the shed and pointed excitedly.

"Here comes your maid, Nan!" she cried. "And there's a man with her. We'll have help now!"

Annie, the Harrison's hired girl, who had been gossiping with the man of all work at the home of the Jamesons, some distance down the street, had seen the smoke from the Harrison house and had hurried to see what was wrong.

Annie was suddenly conscience-stricken and wretchedly frightened.

"And Miss Emma up in that room all by herself and her not able to move hand or foot!" she wailed. "I should 'a' knowed better than to leave her alone, I should! And the worst of the smoke, it's coming from Miss Emma's room!" the half-hysterical Annie wailed, as, followed by the man, she drew nearer. "She's dead by this time! Sure I know it to my sorrow and all the fault o' Annie O'Brien! I wisht I was dead, that I do!"

Nan poked her head over the edge of the shed.

"Stop that noise, Annie! Aunt Emma's safe. And if you've got a good strong man down there, for goodness sake, send him up!"

CHAPTER III

THE RESCUE

The strong man demanded by Nan was forthcoming, the same with whom Annie had been gossiping to the peril of Miss Emma Harrison left alone and helpless in the burning house.

He proved to be an exceedingly strong man, and the girls were lost in admiration at the masterly manner in which he carried Miss Emma down the ladder and placed her in the arms of the penitent Annie.

Annie stood five feet eleven and a half in her stocking feet and was as strong as a man. She held the frail invalid as easily as though she had been a child, and, to do her justice, as tenderly.

Having seen Miss Emma safe, the hired man rejoined the three excited girls on the roof of the shed.

"What's going on here?" he demanded roughly. "Where's the fire?"

"There doesn't seem to be any," said Jo, remembering her bewildered thankfulness over the absence of flames in Aunt Emma's room. "It seems to be all smoke."

"Humph!" grunted the hired man.

He went to the end of the shed and called to some small boys who were beginning to gather. The house was set in a big garden and nobody else was in sight.

"One of you kids run to the next house and send in an alarm to the fire department," he commanded, then returned to where the girls were watching him eagerly.

He took a handkerchief from his pocket and began to tie it over his nose.

"What are you going to do?" demanded Sadie Appleby.

"Don't go in there!" Nan begged, catching the man's arm eagerly. "The house must be all on fire inside! You will be burned to death!"

"If there was flames, you'd have seen 'em before this," the man retorted. He brushed Nan aside, flung a leg over the sill, and the next moment disappeared within the room.

Jo, eager to explore the mystery for herself, was about to follow him recklessly when Nan seized her arm and drew her back.

"No, you don't!" cried the latter. "You have been in danger enough for one day, Jo Morley. Stay where you are!"

Even then Jo might have persisted in her attempt to enter the house, had not her anxiety for the invalid been greater than her curiosity.

"Let's get down to the ground," she proposed. "Maybe we can get into the house by the front way now. And I want to see how your Aunt Emma is, Nan."

Jo scaled down the ladder like the monkey she was on things of the sort, and the other girls followed more slowly.

On reaching the ground they found that the invalid had been taken by Annie down the road to the Jamesons' for first aid.

"But is she alive and all right?" asked Nan, shaking her informant impatiently.

The latter, a lad of about fourteen and conscious of his dignity, replied coldly:

"Oh, she's all right—no thanks to that hired girl of yours though. If I was you, I'd give her the bounce before she's a couple of hours older, that's what I'd do!"

The girls did not stop for further observations on the delinquency of Annie, but joined a group of people who were gathering on the Harrisons' front porch.

Some of these had tried to force their way into the house, but had been driven back by the clouds of smoke.

"Looks like the whole place would go up," one of them said and received a warning glance from the neighbors as Nan and her chums ran up on the porch.

One of the men, an old harness maker, barred the girls' way as they were about to enter the house.

"Better not go in there," said the harness maker, who was a

kindly old man and had long been a pleasant neighbor of the Harrisons'. "There's too much smoke. It would choke you."

"A lot of smoke, but no fire!" cried Nan wonderingly. "I don't understand. Where are the flames?"

Jo, who was beginning to entertain a theory as to the true origin of the smoke, spoke with an air of decision.

"I know one thing, and that is that if the man who went in Aunt Emma's window doesn't come out soon, some one will have to go in and drag him out. He can't stand that smoke very long. I've been in it—and I know!"

"Looks like you'd been down the chimbley," chirped an old man with a wrinkled, parchment-like face and a back bent like a bow. "You got plenty of soot on you, that's one thing sartain, young woman."

"But don't you see? Some one must go in and get that man!" Jo cried desperately. "He may be lying somewhere unconscious this minute. If some one doesn't get him out, he'll die!"

She tried again to get by the man who blocked the doorway.

"Gently, gently!" cried the latter, holding her back. "I'll get him for you, Miss."

The man drew a red-spotted bandana handkerchief from his pocket and began to tie it over his nose and mouth. As he did so a smoke-stained, wild-eyed figure burst through the cloud of smoke and stood swaying in the doorway. At the same moment the clanging of a bell down the road warned all of the approach of the fire engine.

The Jamesons' hired man ripped the handkerchief from over his nose, still holding to the door to steady himself.

"Is it very bad?" cried Nan. "Is the whole house going to burn up?"

The man shook his head.

"'Tain't no fire," he said dully. "Just as I thought. All smoke. Chimney stopped up, back draft, or something."

"Glory be!" cried Sadie. "Make believe that isn't welcome news!"

Nan collapsed, shaking, against the side of the house while

Jo slipped an arm through hers to steady her. Nan began to laugh hysterically.

"Did you hear him, Jo? There isn't any fire. All this f-fuss over n-nothing— —"

"And the fire engines coming!" said Jo, beginning to laugh uncertainly in her turn. "The joke's on some one—either the fire department or us— —"

"Both!" said Sadie. "Here's the hook and ladder, all ready for business! Won't they be disgusted when they learn that the fire's all smoke?"

They were—exceedingly so. The fire chief seemed to consider himself the victim of a practical joke and soon went off down the road in his jangling red car, his back very stiff.

Little the girls cared! Nan, who had expected to see her home go up in flames, fairly danced in the reaction from fear.

Several of the neighbors spoke in a kindly way, offering her and her family the shelter of their homes for the night should the Harrison house prove unfit for occupancy.

Nan thanked them.

"Mother went to a Ladies' Aid meeting this afternoon," she explained. "She should have been home by this time, but I suppose something has happened to detain her. When she comes I'll tell her how kind you've been."

The Jamesons' hired man lingered after the rest of the crowd had dispersed.

"I've opened all the windows to let the smoke out," he told Nan, "and as soon as I can get into the house without smothering, I'd like to have a look at your chimney and fireplaces."

"We have only two," Nan began.

"Chimneys or fireplaces?" asked the hired man, with a chuckle.

"Fireplaces." Nan was patient. "One in the back part of the living room, the other in Aunt Emma's room. I don't know how to thank you," she added gratefully. "You've been awfully good."

"Shucks, I ain't done nothing," declared the man,

embarrassed. "I had a hunch what had happened by the look of the smoke. The chimney must have got all stopped up and some of the soot came down and smothered the fire and sent all the smoke out into the house."

"We ought to go and see how Aunt Emma is," Nan said anxiously, and Sadie called her attention to a small boy running down the road toward them.

"Looks like a messenger from the Jameson place," she said.

"Miss Harrison," the urchin called when he came within hailing distance, "wants to see the girl that saved her life!"

CHAPTER IV

GRATITUDE

The three girl chums stared at each other.

"I guess that means all of us!" said Jo.

Nan ran to meet the boy.

"Is my Aunt Emma all right?" she asked. "She—isn't—Isn't she hurt at all?"

The boy grinned.

"Says she feels better than she has for a long while. Seems like the fright agreed with her!"

Nan hesitated, looking from the boy to the house.

"Some one ought to stay here to break the news to Mother and Dad," she began.

"I'll stay," Jo offered, but the suggestion was instantly shouted down.

"I guess you'll not!" cried Nan. "Aunt Emma wants to see the girl who saved her life, and that girl's name is certainly Jo Morley! You go, Jo!"

"I should say so!" declared Sadie.

The controversy might have lasted some time had not the hired man offered his services.

"I'll wait," he said. "You three run along and never mind the house. I'll take care of everything."

The girls hesitated no longer. Together they started off toward the Jameson house.

On the road they met Annie O'Brien. Annie, though still sheepish and penitent because of her neglect of the invalid, appeared secretly pleased about something.

When stopped and questioned by Nan, however, she would reveal nothing, merely saying that she must hurry on to the house and get supper.

"Rather late in the day to think about it," remarked Sadie. "Seems to me Annie O'Brien had better stick to her job."

"Probably Mother will think something like that," agreed Nan. "Annie likes the hired man," she added. "She makes all sorts of excuses to visit the Jamesons. We've always thought it was funny, but to-day it came near being serious. I suppose because Mother and I were out and Aunt Emma probably dozing in her chair, Annie thought this was a good chance to visit down the street!"

"I hate to think what would have happened if there had been fire as well as smoke," said Jo, with a shudder.

"My, but you were brave, Jo," said Sadie admiringly. "Just jumped through the window without a thought of what might happen to you on the other side."

"I was thinking of Miss Emma," Jo said simply.

"And then, when you stayed in the room, we made sure something terrible had happened and came after you," Nan said.

"Something terrible nearly did happen, both to your Aunt Emma and me," returned Jo, with a rueful smile.

"I know, and you can better believe Aunt Emma will hear the whole of it. You won't lose anything, Jo."

"Now, listen!" Jo said, alarmed. "If you are going to try to make me out a heroine or any silly thing like that, I'm going home right now— —"

"Try to do it!" laughed Nan.

She had one of Jo's arms in hers, and at the words Sadie grasped the other.

"You are both bigger than I," said Jo, in her best tragedy-queen manner. "You know that I have no chance to escape, brutes that you are!"

The chums soon reached the Jamesons' gate, and as they pushed it open Mrs. Jameson herself came out of the house and beckoned to them.

Her face was alight with that same mysterious glow that the girls had noticed on Annie's countenance.

"Aunt Emma?" Nan queried anxiously. "Is she all right, Mrs. Jameson?"

The latter nodded, finger to lips. She was a handsome woman in her late thirties, tall and graceful, and with hair that was almost white. Her interest in the invalid at the Harrison house was as great as it was genuine. She was a familiar figure at the house down the street and spent many an afternoon with Miss Emma, telling her the news of the town or reading light literature as the latter's mood required.

At a loss to understand the look of happiness on the face of this good neighbor, Nan would have questioned her further but that Mrs. Jameson forestalled her.

"Come in and see your Aunt Emma for yourself," she said.

Mrs. Jameson of course knew Nan's chums, so that no introduction was necessary.

The girls followed the lady of the house into the big front room that was library and sitting room combined.

Miss Emma was propped up in a big easy chair, cushions beneath her, cushions behind her head, and cushions under her feet. She looked by no means as white and weary as the girls had feared to find her. On the contrary, her eyes were bright and there was an unusual tinge of color in her face.

Nan ran to her and flung an arm about the frail shoulders.

"Oh, Aunt Emma, I'm so thankful you are safe! When we heard you cry out from your room and knew that you were in the burning house alone we were horribly frightened!"

"I know!" Miss Emma stroked the fair head gently with a thin, blue-veined hand. "But I am all right now. So don't cry, dear. Yes, you are crying!" The thin hand went beneath Nan's chin and turned the girl's face up, revealing an April face upon which tears and smiles were intermingled.

"Here, take my handkerchief and stop that, child! There's nothing in the world to cry about!" Nan accepted the handkerchief and hugged her aunt again in thankfulness for her safety.

Sadie and Jo were standing just within the doorway, uncomfortably watching the intimate scene.

"Let's run away!" Jo whispered to Sadie. "They don't know we're here!"

But in this Nan's Aunt Emma immediately proved her wrong.

"I want to know who it was came into my room and carried me to the window," she said in a voice that, for her, was unusually determined. "I thought it was Nan, but now I realize it wasn't her voice I heard at all."

"Jo did it, Aunt Emma," Nan said before Jo, backing hastily to the door, could escape. "She was wonderful! She told us where to put the ladder and then swarmed up it like a little monkey."

"Oh, hush, Nan, please!" cried Jo, who hated above all things to be praised.

"I won't hush!" cried Nan. "Aunt Emma asked a question, and certainly she has a right to know who saved her life!"

"I didn't!" protested Jo. "When you and Sadie reached me I was about all in."

"And why?" retorted Nan. "Because you risked your life—that's why!"

Mrs. Jameson smiled as Miss Harrison, eyes bright, beckoned Jo to come closer.

Jo knelt beside the invalid's chair and put a strong, tanned hand over Miss Emma's thin one.

"I didn't do anything, really—although I tried to," she protested. "You fainted— —"

"Yes, I remember that, now!"

"And I managed to carry you as far as the window. But it was lucky that Sadie and Nan were there, for I could never have lifted you to the shed roof alone."

"I owe a great debt to all you girls," the invalid said slowly. "But I owe a little more to you, my dear, because you risked your life so gallantly and fearlessly to save mine. I wish there were something I could do to show you how I feel, Jo Morley."

"You can try to get well, if you please," said Jo with one of her quick smiles. "That would please me better than anything else!"

"Which reminds me, Miss Emma," broke in the soft voice of Mrs. Jameson, "that you have not yet told the girls your great news!"

The girls looked wonderingly from Miss Harrison to Mrs. Jameson, then back to the former again.

Miss Emma's face flushed. She made a motion as though to rise from her chair. She was trembling suddenly with an almost childish excitement.

"At the moment I heard Jo's voice in the room," she said swiftly, "I tried to struggle to my feet. In one great effort I did raise myself! For a moment I stood upon my feet!"

CHAPTER V

A STARTLING REVELATION

The girl chums were speechless, staring at the flushed face of the woman before them.

If it had not been for Mrs. Jameson, smiling behind the invalid's chair, they might have thought Miss Harrison was still suffering from shock and unable to comprehend the staggering importance of this statement.

Why, for years, Emma Harrison had been confined to her chair, the lower part of her body absolutely helpless. Yet just now she had said, and with every appearance of sincerity, that only a short time before she had actually stood upon her feet!

"Aunt Emma!" cried Nan incredulously, "do you know what you are saying?"

"Oh, I can't blame you for not believing me," replied Miss Emma, speaking in the same swift, excited manner. "I don't know how I did it. I don't even know that I could do it again. But one thing I do know—that for a moment I stood unaided, firmly, upon my two feet!"

"That's wonderful!" cried Jo eagerly. "If you did it once, you can surely do it again if you try."

"But not for some time yet," protested Mrs. Jameson, fearful lest the enthusiasm of the girls lead the invalid on to a second and unwise attempt to try her new power. "Your aunt has had a very dreadful experience, Nan, and I think what she now needs most is rest and quiet. I propose, with your mother's consent, to keep her with me for the night."

"You are always so kind," Nan said gratefully. "I think it would be best not to try to move her again to-night, especially back to our dismal, smoke-grimed house," and she grimaced distastefully at thought of what her family would have to put up with until the chimney could be repaired and the traces of smoke erased.

"I think you had all better stay here for the night," Mrs. Jameson suggested hospitably. "Hurry home and see what your mother says, my dear. Mr. Jameson and I will be glad to have you."

This was evidently dismissal, and all three girls thought they could guess the reason for it.

Aunt Emma was as eager as a child to discuss her wonderful experience—the fact that after all these years she had been able, if only for a moment, to stand unaided upon her feet.

As for the girls, a flood of queries trembled upon their tongues. If permitted, they would have questioned the invalid far more than was good for her. Mrs. Jameson saw this and was bent upon placing both them and Miss Emma beyond the reach of temptation.

But before they went the invalid called Jo over to her.

"You are a good brave girl," she said, holding Jo's sunburned hand in hers for a moment. "If there is anything you want very much, ever, let me know and I will get it for you if it is at all within my power."

On impulse Jo bent down and kissed the flushed cheek.

"Just get well! That's all I ask of you!" she said.

When they were out in the street again, having said good-bye to Mrs. Jameson, the girls were somewhat thoughtful.

"Do you think your Aunt Emma will ever be able to walk again?" asked Sadie Appleby. "Do you think it meant anything, her standing alone there for a moment when she heard Jo's voice?"

"I don't know," Nan returned slowly. "She was excited, of course, and soon afterward she fainted. There might have been a good deal of imagination in what she said."

"I don't think so." Jo shook her head and her brow was creased in an effort to think clearly. "I was half-blinded by the smoke and it was dark in the room when I stumbled across your Aunt Emma's chair, Nan. A moment later I felt my arms about some one, but I can't tell for the life of me whether that some one was standing up or seated in the chair. I took it for granted that she was sitting down—but I might have been mistaken."

"Well, anyway, it will do a lot of good if she only thinks she can use her feet," Nan decided. "It will give her hope, and that's what she has been without for a good long time. Poor Aunt Emma!"

The girl chums had come by this time to the Harrison house. There were lights inside and Nan could see that her father and mother had reached home and had learned of the damage done during their absence.

"You can come in for a few minutes and say hello to Mother, can't you?" Nan urged, but the other girls demurred.

"I'll have to run along or the folks will think I'm lost, strayed, or stolen for good this time," Sadie laughed.

"Same here!" Jo's face was sober, almost sad, and Nan thought she knew what was wrong.

"You're worrying about Laurel Hall, Jo," she said sympathetically. "But don't get too blue. There must be a way out, if only we can find it."

"If only we can find it!" repeated Jo, with a wry little twist of her lips. "So long, Nan. See you to-morrow."

As Sadie and Jo went on toward the center of town where they lived on the same street in houses across one from the other, they were both subdued and thoughtful.

"It's hard luck for us all." Sadie spoke the thought that she knew was in Jo's mind too. "Just when we had come so close to it! Why, Jo, do you realize that in two weeks we were to start for Laurel Hall?"

Jo gave a little laugh that was part sob.

"I haven't been realizing anything else since last night!" she said.

The girls reached Jo's gate and lingered before it a moment, turning their faces to the crisp evening breeze.

Suddenly Jo caught Sadie's hand in hers and squeezed it passionately.

"You're going—you and Nan!" she said in a fierce little whisper. "I'm not a—a dog in the manger, Sade!"

There was the noise of a clicking gate latch and Jo sped up the path to the house.

Sadie sighed and made her way slowly across the road to her own home. The pleasant aroma of cooking things greeted her from the open door. It was then that Sadie made a discovery. For the first time in her healthy young life she had lost her appetite!

The news of Jo's heroism had reached home before her. Mrs. Morley, a plump, comfortable woman of forty, greeted her daughter at the door with a flood of proud, motherly questions.

Jo, who was feeling suddenly very weary and discouraged, almost on the point of tears, answered apathetically:

"There wasn't anything to my part of it, Mother dear, really." She followed her mother to the pleasantly lighted dining room. "The Jameson man thinks the chimney was clogged up or that part of it fell in, smothering the fires in the grates and driving the smoke out into the house," she continued. "There wasn't any great damage done. Probably in a day or two the Harrisons will forget that it ever happened."

She looked about the cheerful dining room. Food was set on the table—tempting food, the kind her efficient, comfortable mother always provided—but Mr. Morley was nowhere to be seen.

"Hasn't Dad come home yet?" asked Jo, as she glanced without enthusiasm at the tempting viands.

Mrs. Morley's rosy face clouded. She looked worried and harassed and her fingers twitched nervously at the corners of her napkin.

"He is down at the office, trying to straighten things out—"

At the sound of the opening door she broke off suddenly and put a finger to her lips.

"Here he is now," she said in a low voice. "We must try to cheer him, Jo dear. He has a great deal to worry him these days."

Jo looked up as her father came slowly and heavily into the room. She was surprised and shocked to see how dreadfully he had aged in the past twenty-four hours. How could so short a time work so much mischief?

With a dazed expression Mr. Morley's eyes wandered about the familiar room. He seemed hardly to see his wife and daughter who looked at him with compassionate eyes. He appeared old—old and broken.

Suddenly Jo forgot herself in pity for her father.

She sprang to her feet and put an arm about him and pushed him gently into his chair.

"Poor old Dad!" she said softly. "You've had a pretty rough time of it, haven't you? I—we're so sorry, dear."

CHAPTER VI

A SCOUNDREL

If anything could break through her father's state of dazed misery, Jo Morley's sympathy was that thing.

Mr. Morley sank into his chair at the table and buried his tired face in his hands.

"You're a good girl, Jo," he said, and, reaching up, patted the hand that rested on his shoulder. "I'm a little tired, that's all. I'll be better after I've had something to eat."

Catching Jo's eye, Mrs. Morley gestured to her and the girl slipped noiselessly into her seat.

They unostentatiously served the meal, chatting pleasantly the while until Mr. Morley raised his head and looked about him with more animation.

Jo, seeing that her chatter lightened the general gloom, entered into a whimsical account of the afternoon's doing that appeared to interest her father.

"What a tragedy it might have been!" cried Mrs. Morley. "That poor helpless Emma Harrison alone in her room, unable to save herself!"

"It was lucky for her that our Jo happened along," said Mr. Morley, smiling.

"And Nan Harrison and Sadie Appleby!" Jo retorted. "They had as much to do with the rescue as I, remember!"

Mr. Morley knew better than to argue with Jo's obstinate conviction, but he shook his head and smiled to himself as if to say that he had his own ideas on that subject!

It was only after dinner was over and the dishes cleared away that Mr. Morley's deep depression returned.

When Mrs. Morley went upstairs to get some mending, Jo wandered into the library and saw her father seated in his favorite easy chair, the very picture of discouragement.

In the doorway Jo hesitated, then went swiftly forward and seated herself on the arm of her father's chair.

She ran her fingers through his graying, curly hair, a caressing habit that had been hers since she was a very small child.

Mr. Morley looked up at her sadly.

"Such a good girl, Josie," he said, "deserves the best of everything."

Jo put a hand over his mouth.

"Don't let's talk about me," she wheedled. "I want to talk about you."

Mr. Morley sighed heavily and turned his gaze once more toward the fire that burned in the grate.

There was a long silence broken only by the snapping of the blazing logs. Then Jo ventured softly:

"I wish you would tell me just what is wrong in your business, Dad. I don't think I quite understand."

"It's hard for older heads than yours to understand, Jo," returned her father. "How a trusted employee of a company can deliberately betray the secrets of that company and ruin his employer— —"

"Oh, so it's a man who has made all the trouble!" Jo cried impulsively.

"A man who is either a maniac or one of the most contemptible scoundrels alive," her father returned bitterly. "The name of the scoundrel is Andrew Simmer, and he was my trusted clerk. You've seen him. You know what he looks like."

"What—what happened to him?" queried Jo, after another interval of unhappy silence.

"He decamped with some of the company's money and bonds," said Mr. Morley, speaking harshly despite his great fatigue. "And for the rest, he has left the company's affairs in such an involved condition that it looks as if utter ruin stretched before me."

"Ruin!" Jo repeated incredulously. "You mean we shall have—no money—at all?"

Mr. Morley glanced up at the girl and his face was haggard. He made a gesture of denial.

"I should not have said so much," he said after a pause and in a changed tone. "I am tired to-night and probably things seem worse to me than they actually are. We won't talk about it any more, poor Jo, poor little Jo."

Jo almost cried after that, and to save adding her tears to her father's already heavy burden ran from his presence up to her room where she buried her face in the pillows and wept long and furiously.

"That Andrew Simmer!" she cried, clenching her fist angrily. "What a scoundrel he must be! No wonder Dad looks savage when he speaks of him!"

Jo went downstairs no more that night, and when her mother came to her to ask why she did not join the family group as usual in the library, Jo pleaded a headache and said that she was going to bed.

She went to bed but not to sleep—not for many long hours afterward. In fact, the first shadowy light of dawn was creeping in at her windows before she fell into an uneasy, dream-tormented sleep.

The result was that Jo slept late and did not come downstairs until her father had been gone for some time. This was just as well, she thought, since her father could scarcely fail to notice the signs left by her sleepless night, the shadows under her eyes, the pallor of her cheeks. This would worry him and Jo wished more than anything in the world not to add to his burden of trouble just then.

From her mother Jo learned the rest of the story concerning Andrew Simmer.

"He seems to have been an extraordinarily clever young man," Mrs. Morley explained. "There are those who say now, in the light of later events, that he was more crafty and cunning than clever. Some even go so far as to say they think he was a bit touched in the head."

"Crazy?" asked Jo, her eyes intent upon her mother's face.

"I don't know as to that. But the fact remains that Simmer was clever, or crafty, enough to find out for himself some of the secrets of the business that your father has kept carefully guarded from every one else."

"Did he take much money?" Jo asked breathlessly.

"I was coming to that." There was something of rebuke in Mrs. Morley's tone. "He found out—how, nobody knows—the combination of the office safe. After that it was an easy matter to take what he could find of negotiable paper and money and decamp with it."

"He's gone, then? Run away?" cried Jo.

"Disappeared overnight, leaving no trace behind him," returned Mrs. Morley, distress again clouding the usual good nature of her face. "Your father has notified the police, of course, and set detectives on his trail; but so far without result. It actually looks as if the earth had opened and swallowed him up."

"Which of course it hasn't," muttered Jo, thinking her thought aloud.

"What did you say, dear," queried Mrs. Morley.

"I was just wondering," Jo returned vaguely. "Andrew Simmer must be somewhere, and since that's true, the detectives are sure to find him sooner or later."

"Probably later," returned her mother pessimistically. "And so much later that it won't do your father much good. He will be hopelessly ruined long before that time."

Jo paled, and, as she did so, remembered her father's haggard face as it was lifted to hers the night before in the library.

"Mother, is that what Dad—what all of us—are facing—actual ruin?"

Mrs. Morley hesitated, then turned her steady, kindly gaze upon her daughter.

"I don't see any reason why you should not know the truth, Jo," she said. "In fact, I think it is your right to know. We may lose everything we have in the world, dear."

As she spoke she put her arm about the girl's tense shoulders.

"This house?" asked Jo, in a voice scarcely above a whisper.

Mrs. Morley nodded.

"I'm afraid so, honey."

Jo was silent for so long a time that Mrs. Morley looked at her anxiously.

At last the girl spoke.

"What will Dad do?"

"Start all over again, I suppose—at the bottom," came wearily from her mother. "What else can he do?"

"Poor Dad," said Jo, the tears stinging her eyes. "It will be mighty hard on him. We—we've got to help him, Mother, you and I."

Mrs. Morley's grip about Jo's shoulders tightened.

"I am glad you take it this way, dear," she said. "Your father will need all the help we can give him." After a short pause she added: "I think one of the greatest trials he has to bear just now is that he can't send you to Laurel Hall. He has counted on it—almost as much as you have, I think."

Jo's lips quivered.

"There—there's some one on the porch, I think," she said and, rising, hastily left the room.

This was a mere pretense on Jo's part in order to get away from her mother before the latter saw how much the disappointment meant to her. But when Jo reached her front door she saw that some one actually was on the porch.

Nan and Sadie were there, arm in arm, and Sadie was in the act of ringing the bell when Jo forestalled her by opening the door in person.

"Hello! Just the person we want to see!"

There was a joyful ring in Nan's voice that jarred upon Jo's mood of depression.

"Go get your hat," Sadie added. "It's too nice a day to waste in the house. We're going for a walk."

"All right," said Jo, and turned back into the house to get her hat, all unsuspecting of what was in store for her.

CHAPTER VII

THE SURPRISE

Sadie Appleby and Nan Harrison waited below stairs, chatting with Mrs. Morley while in her room above Jo crushed a felt hat over her dark hair and regarded her reflection with an air of discouragement.

"You look like a wreck," she told her mirrored self. "If you could get a little color in your face you might not look quite so much like a ghost."

As Jo reached the head of the stairs she paused for a moment to listen to the merry chatter of Nan and Sadie. Despite herself she felt hurt that they should feel so gay when they could not help knowing how downhearted she must be. Yesterday they had seemed to care whether she went to Laurel Hall with them or not. To-day they appeared quite reconciled to her staying home. Was it possible that Nan and Sadie, the two chums from whom she had rarely ever been separated during their years of work and fun together, should care so little for her as their manner seemed to imply? If they did not care, then she would show them that neither did she!

Jo shrugged her shoulders impatiently and forced a smile to her quivering lips. She must not—must not!—allow herself to become morbid!

So it was a rather strained though smiling Jo who met her friends at the foot of the stairs.

"All right, let's go," she said. "We won't be gone long, Mother. Is there anything," as an afterthought, "that you need at the store?"

Mrs. Morley mentioned one or two articles, and Jo promised to bring them home with her when she returned.

"How is your Aunt Emma?" Jo asked of Nan when they were once outside the house.

"Amazingly fine!" Nan rejoined. "We have had the doctor in to see her this morning, Jo, and he says that there is a wonderful improvement in her. She seems to have taken a new hold on life and a new interest in it."

"Oh, I'm glad!" cried Jo. "Wouldn't it be wonderful if she got well after all?"

"She simply dotes on you," Sadie told her. "Nan says she talks of no one else."

"And she wants to see you again this morning," Nan added.

Jo frowned.

"I'd love to see her, of course. But if she is going to thank me again— —"

"Nothing like that," Nan assured her buoyantly. "She just wants to see you. Says it would brighten her up."

It was on the tip of Jo's tongue to say that it would be hard for her to brighten any one up on that particular morning, but pride forbade the words. If the girls had forgotten so soon the change in her affairs that was nothing less than tragedy to her, then she would not remind them of it!

She permitted her companions to lead her to the Harrison house, the scene of all the excitement the previous afternoon.

"The fire was a false alarm in more senses than one," said Nan, as she opened the gate. "The Jamesons' hired man cleared out the chimney for us, and except for the dirt and the smoke grime on the woodwork, the house is as good as ever. Even Aunt Emma's room isn't hurt," she added, "although we've put her in the big front room until the paint can be washed and her room made presentable again."

Jo felt numb and dazed, almost as her father must have felt when he reached home the night before. It was so hard to pretend to be cheerful and matter-of-fact when one's world was falling to pieces about one's feet! She wanted to run away and hide herself in a corner and be openly just as miserable as she felt.

But Sadie's arm was linked in hers. She would have to go on pretending to be cheerful for a little while yet.

Her two chums took her up to the sunny front room where Miss Emma was sitting, her face brighter than Jo ever remembered it.

Mrs. Harrison, seated beside the invalid, came forward as Jo entered the room and kissed the girl affectionately.

"We owe you a great debt of gratitude, my dear," she said. "And now," with a glance over her shoulder at Miss Emma, "this lady has a request to make of you."

"A request?" Jo echoed, wondering.

She looked toward the two girls as though for an explanation. Both Nan and Sadie were smiling, and now Nan pushed her forward impatiently.

"Can't you see the lady wants to speak to you?" Sadie cried. "Don't stand there staring like a ninny, Jo Morley!"

Miss Emma motioned with her thin hand to a place on the window seat beside her chair.

"After what happened yesterday, I wanted to learn all about you, my dear— —"

"Indeed, she asked me about six million questions!" Nan interjected.

"Naturally I wanted to find out about the girl that saved my life." Miss Emma made a quick imperative gesture as Jo would have interrupted. "And I found out many things; among them," instinctively the invalid's voice lowered, "that this girl, or rather her family, was in serious trouble."

Jo nodded and turned her face away. Just then she could not trust herself to speak.

"And what I want that girl to do," Aunt Emma continued while the spectators of the little scene drew closer to the two chief actors in it, "is to let me help, to try to repay the great debt I owe her."

As Jo looked up, wondering and a little startled, Miss Emma's hand covered hers.

"If your father's business is so involved that he can't see his way clear just now to sending you to Laurel Hall boarding school with Nan and Sadie," Miss Emma hurried on, "then I want you to let me take his place just now. I want you to let me send you instead. You will let me do that, won't you, dear?"

Jo's heart leaped with sudden hope, even while she felt that she could not accept so generous an offer. She was about to protest when she caught a warning glance from Nan, who was stationed behind the invalid's chair.

"Don't cross her!" was what Nan telegraphed. "It might prove serious!"

Jo, flustered, hardly knowing what reply to make, found herself looking straight into Miss Emma's kindly, questioning eyes.

"The favor would be to me, my dear," Miss Harrison continued. "It is a long time since I have been able to do anything for any one. If I thought I had helped to make you happy, who have done so much for me, that thought would give me a new interest in life, I think. You want to go to Laurel Hall, don't you?"

The blood rushed to Jo's face, her eyes shone.

"Want to go!" she cried. Suddenly she saw her way clear before her. "Oh, Miss Emma, you don't know how much I want to go! How wonderfully good and kind you are to me! I will never forget it! Never!"

Clinging to the eager girl, Miss Emma seemed to draw strength from the contact with glowing youth. Sitting there, sharing in the general rejoicing, she looked younger than she had looked for years.

"It would have been cruel to have refused her, Jo."

It was some time later and the chums were on their way to Jo's home to make definite plans for their departure for Laurel Hall.

In reply to Nan's observation Jo nodded.

"She had her heart set on it, and what a good heart she has! Imagine her wanting to send me away to school just because I was able to help a little yesterday. And, after all, what did I do?"

"Plenty, Miss Emma thinks," chuckled Sadie, and added with a gesture toward the Morley house: "There's your mother on the porch. Are you going to break the glad news to her now?"

"I'll say I am!"

Jo ran up the path to the house, took the porch steps two at a time, seized Mrs. Morley by the hands, and whirled her about until that lady scarcely knew which was her head and which her heels—at least, so she said.

"Mother!" cried Jo, "I've got a surprise for you! Something wonderful has happened! You will never guess what!"

"You'd better tell me," suggested her mother practically. "I can see you're bursting with it."

"Well, then, listen! I'm going to Laurel Hall, after all!"

CHAPTER VIII

OFF FOR LAUREL HALL

When Mrs. Morley learned that Jo's statement was not a product of her imagination, but the sober truth, she looked grave.

"I don't know whether your father will want any one else to send you to school, my dear," she said slowly.

It took the girls some time to win her over to their viewpoint, but Nan, speaking eloquently, drew a word picture of the life of her invalid aunt with the object of showing how hurt, and perhaps seriously affected, mentally and physically, the latter would be should her well meant proposal be rejected. In the end Mrs. Morley was led to believe that Miss Emma would suffer more than Jo if the latter were not allowed to go to Laurel Hall!

"Well, maybe you're right," said the girl's mother at last reluctantly. "But I don't know whether your father will see it that way, Jo."

"It's up to you to make him see it that way, Mother dear," said Jo and kissed her mother pleadingly. "You can, you know!"

In the end Mr. Morley was won over, as Jo had felt sure he would be. It was definitely decided that Jo was to go to Laurel Hall.

On the night that he made his decision and gave Jo permission to accept Miss Emma's generosity, Mr. Morley left the room for a moment and returned with a pitifully small roll of bank bills.

These he thrust into Jo's hand without looking at her.

"Get yourself some clothes, Josie," he said a bit huskily. "It won't go very far, but it may do for the present and I'll try to send you more later."

Jo looked at the little roll of bills, knowing how tragically hard it was to part with even so small a sum in these hard days of threatened financial ruin.

She went up to her father and plucked him by the sleeve.

"I—I don't need this, Dad," she said bravely. "What clothes I have will do."

But Mr. Morley shook his head, still without looking at her. Jo noticed his eyes looked heavy and bloodshot—as though he had not slept for a long time.

"You've got to have it," he said, almost bruskly. "I only wish I could make it ten times as much!"

Mr. Morley had admitted that could the absconding clerk, Andrew Simmer, be found and brought to justice, something might yet be saved from the threatened wreck of his business.

But Andrew Simmer was gone, "disappeared overnight," her mother had said, "as though the earth had opened and swallowed him up."

As each day with its excited preparations brought the three girls nearer to the opening of the boarding school and their departure for Laurelton, Jo caught the contagion of Sadie's and Nan's excitement and forgot to some extent the unhappiness at home.

At last the day before the great event arrived. Sadie and Nan had shopped steadily—Jo, too, to the limit of the thin little bank roll.

Miss Emma, sharing in the pleasurable excitement of the girls, would have supplied Jo with everything she needed, furnished her with a complete wardrobe, but here Mr. Morley resolutely drew the line.

"If Jo can't go with the clothes I can give her, then she cannot go at all," he said, and Jo assured him with tears in her eyes that she was perfectly content with what she had, that, indeed, she had not wanted to take anything even from him under the circumstances!

So it came to pass that Jo's trunk was packed long before Nan and Sadie had finished buying pretty things. Jo had steeled herself to do without a great many things that she had expected to have and could have had if it had not been for Andrew Simmer, rascal.

"I've a score to settle with that fellow," she thought vengefully. "If I should ever meet him!"

But her chief worry was for her mother and father. Both were dreadfully downcast and there were times when Jo felt that she should not leave them at all.

"If by staying at home I could do any good!" was the way she argued it to herself. "If I could do any good I wouldn't stir a step! But I would only be moping about all the time, making things ten times worse, probably. Anyway, I know Dad is glad I am to have Laurel Hall after all, though he hates to think of any one else paying my way there. Poor Dad! If there were only something I could do to help!"

When, the evening before they were to start, Jo and Sadie ran over to Nan's home for a few minutes happy talk on the prospects of the morrow, they found Nan just packing a new sport sweater and her tennis racket.

"I've got a new one," Sadie said, pointing to the racket. "Dad brought one home to-night—a perfect peach! He said he would buy me a new one every season if it would improve my game."

"Evidently he doesn't think much of your game!" laughed Nan.

Sadie made a face at her.

"Neither do you, you horrid girl," she accused. "Stop laughing, or I'll throw something at you."

"As the thing nearest at hand is the brass umbrella holder, I'd advise you to do as she says!" chuckled Jo.

The joke was well understood among the chums, who were all three ardent lovers of the game of tennis. But whereas Jo and Nan had profited by steady and conscientious practice and were by way of becoming exceptionally good players, especially Nan, Sadie seemed to lack something—speed or muscle or quick judgment—that goes to the making of a good tennis player.

But Sadie continued to practice doggedly and still lived in

hope that some day she would be able to beat Jo—or even Nan! But that day, even in Sadie's rueful judgment, was a long way off.

"How about you, Jo?" Nan asked, looking across at the dark-haired girl. "It seemed to me last time we were on the courts that your racket looked a bit seedy. Don't you need a new one?"

"I need lots of things I'm not going to get," said Jo and smiled bravely and skillfully changed the subject.

Before the girls left Jo went up to see Miss Emma and found her still much more cheerful and hopeful than she had been before the fire scare.

When Jo was leaving Miss Harrison told her to put her hand behind the door in the corner of the room and see what she could find there.

Jo obeyed and drew forth a beautiful new racket and a set of balls!

The girl could not speak for a moment, but kept turning the handsome racket over and over in her hands, her eyes misty.

"You are very good to me, Miss Emma," she said at last. "How can I ever repay you?"

"I am very busy repaying you!" laughed Miss Emma, her eyes bright.

Some time later Sadie and Jo walked home through the moonlight in a happy mood.

"Laurel Hall to-morrow," said Sadie in a solemn voice, stopping at her gate.

"Laurel Hall forever!" responded Jo, a lilt in her voice. "And I've got a new tennis racket, Sade! Make believe I won't wallop everybody in sight!"

"Except Nan," said Sadie.

"Maybe—except Nan," Jo conceded. "See you to-morrow, Sade. Nine o'clock, sharp!"

The girls were ready at considerably before nine o'clock the following morning. Although each solemnly declared that she had not slept at all, the honest fact was that they had slept uncommonly well and had only been aroused to the important facts of the day by the insistent ringing of three alarm clocks set at three respective bedsides.

Be that as it may, the fact remains that they were all ready with grips packed and hats on, a full half hour before it was time to start for the station.

"We may as well go anyway," Nan argued, as they met on the Morleys' porch. "The train might be early, you know. And suppose we should miss it?"

They all agreed that this would be nothing short of tragic.

"Dad will take us down," said Sadie. "See, he's backing the car out of the garage now."

So the girls and their baggage and Mr. and Mrs. Morley piled into the Appleby auto—which was considerably crowded when they were all accommodated—and started off at a great pace for the station.

"Off at last!" cried Nan. "Girls, I'd begun to think this moment never would come!"

CHAPTER IX

KATE SPEED

The train which the three Woodford girls were to take went to Waterville, at the head of Twin Mountain Lake. It was upon this picturesque body of water that the boarding school of Laurel Hall was situated. On reaching Waterville the girls must take a steamer to Laurelton, which was a village about six miles down the lake.

Twin Mountain Lake was about fifteen miles long and a mile in width, and the fact that it lay in a valley between two mountains was responsible for its name.

The lake was famous for its picturesque beauty. The shoreline was irregular and much indented, and small islands were scattered through it in a way to add to its mystery and charm.

No wonder the girl chums were anxious to reach romantic Laurel Hall, situated as it was in the most exquisite of natural settings.

There was quite a crowd gathered at the Woodford station when the train that was to carry the schoolgirls to Waterville steamed into it.

Mr. Morley and Mr. Appleby boarded the car with the girls, to carry their luggage and see them safely installed for the journey. When this was done a tremor of the train warned them that they must seek the platform with as little delay as possible.

Jo caught her father's coat as he turned to go.

"I'll be thinking of you and Mother all the time, Dad," she said in a hurried whisper. "And I'm going to pray that you get hold of that Andrew Simmer one way or another!"

Mr. Morley gave a wry smile and patted her hand.

"Let's hope I shall!" he said. Then he had to jump to reach the platform as the train moved off.

The girls peered through the windows and waved hands and handkerchiefs until the familiar faces were blurred by distance.

"Well, we're off!" said Nan, turning her head and regarding her chums with dancing eyes. "I've had a horrible feeling we'd never get to Laurel Hall ever since Jo scared us to death by saying she couldn't go."

"We're not there yet," Sadie reminded her, with a grin. "There's always the chance of a train wreck, you know."

"How cheerful! Sadie has such a lovely way of looking on the sunny side of things!" Jo was about to make further remarks in the same strain when her words were arrested by the inquiring glance of a girl in the next seat.

She was an expensively dressed girl—almost flashily dressed—and as Jo's eyes met hers she smiled and came over to the double seat in which the three girl chums were comfortably settled.

"I couldn't help overhearing what you said," she began in a high, mincing voice. "Is it possible that you are going to Laurel Hall, too?"

"Too," thought the girls. Was this flashily dressed, affected young person by any chance a fellow student?

"That's certainly the place we're bound for," returned Jo, as the questioner's eyes remained fixed on her.

"We're just entering," Sadie added.

Nan said nothing. She was busy forming an instinctive and intense dislike of the stranger.

"How lucky!" cried the latter effusively. "I'm a student at Laurel Hall, too—second year. How nice we should meet like this on the train!"

"Yes, isn't it!" said Nan, though the faint tinge of sarcasm passed unnoticed by the new girl.

"Won't you sit down?" asked Sadie, who was always polite, even to those for whom she did not care greatly.

"Just a moment," said the strange girl. "I have a friend here. I'll ask her if she won't join us."

"By all means!" Nan muttered as the girl turned away. "Why not invite the whole train? There's room for all!"

Jo choked on a laugh and raised a hand in warning to Nan. Their new friend was already returning. Another girl was with her.

This girl was introduced as Lily Darrow and the girl chums liked her at once. Lily Darrow was a quiet, sweet-faced young person with light brown hair and light brown eyes and a soft voice that seemed always just above a whisper.

Lily took the seat next to Nan while the girl whom they now knew by the name of Kate Speed perched herself on the arm of the seat beside Jo.

Kate had hair that was so fair it was almost white. Her eyebrows were of the same color and were about as much use to her as though she had had none at all. Her eyes were a deep violet blue and, being heavily lashed, saved her from that washed-out appearance so unattractive in any one.

Her clothes, which the Woodford girls had already briefly commented on, were as noticeable as her eyes, and made Kate Speed a conspicuous figure wherever she went.

"Too bad you haven't been to Laurel Hall before," she rattled on to the slightly bored girls. "Such a nuisance, getting acquainted, don't you think so? I felt frightfully out of things my first term. But now, of course, it's quite different. I may be able to do a lot for you girls, introducing you to the right people and all that," she added patronizingly.

The chums exchanged a glance, half amused, half annoyed.

"Thanks, so much," said Nan gravely. "I know we should never have been able to get along without you."

Kate Speed looked at her suspiciously, as though she detected sarcasm beneath the flattering statement. But Nan's face still wore its look of innocent gravity and Kate Speed rattled on in a more egotistic vein than ever.

"Laurel Hall is a lovely school and all that, and I really never would care to go anywhere else. There's only one fault I have to find with it."

"What's that?" asked Sadie, simulating a breathless interest.

"It's too cliquish," explained Kate, with a toss of her light head. "If the girls don't know all about you and your family, they are apt to be a bit stand-offish."

"Oh, Kate, do you think so?" Lily Darrow's protest was timid. "I've always thought the girls at Laurel Hall were the friendliest in the world."

"Well, of course, if you think so, Lily Darrow, that settles it!" Again Kate Speed tossed her head and looked daggers at the timid girl.

Lily flushed and murmured something about "not meaning to contradict."

"You didn't mean to contradict! Well, I'd like to know what you did mean!" scolded Kate. "After this, Lily Darrow, I'll thank you to keep your opinions to yourself!"

Sadie, Nan, and Jo exchanged amazed glances. Who was this Kate Speed that she could talk to another girl, a student at Laurel Hall, in such a manner?

"And get away with it," Jo added later when they were alone. It was nearing lunch time, and Kate Speed and her companion had gone back to the dining car, leaving the three chums to the enjoyment of the sandwiches, fruit, and cake prepared by loving hands at home. Kate had tossed her head at sight of the homely lunch baskets and had hinted that she was far above dining in such a manner aboard a train! "Why, Kate Speed seems to own that girl body and soul!"

"She has some hold over her, that's a sure thing," Sadie agreed.

"Well, I feel sorry for any one in the power of that fair-haired cat," said Nan almost spitefully. She had conceived a tremendous dislike for their flashy new acquaintance.

"I scent a mystery here," remarked Jo, who was always scenting mysteries everywhere, "and I'm willing to bet that we'll be able to solve it before we've been at Laurel Hall very long."

"If we can rescue Lily Darrow from the clutches of Speedy Kate, we'll have done one good day's work," said Nan.

The girls chuckled.

"'Speedy Kate,'" laughed Jo. "That's a good one, Nan. Just fits her."

And by the name of "Speedy Kate" the fair-haired girl was known to the three chums of Woodford from that time on.

The rest of the trip to Waterville, upon which the girls had counted so much, was practically spoiled for them by the persistent company of Kate Speed and her meek little companion.

When the long train journey was nearing its close and they were speeding on to Waterville, the next stop, Nan happened to mention the fact that she played tennis.

"How nice!" cried Kate Speed. "You'll find I have quite a reputation on the courts at Laurel Hall. I'll take you on whenever you say," with a challenging look at Nan, "and wallop you with the greatest of pleasure!"

CHAPTER X

THE CHALLENGE

Nan Harrison met the insolent look of Kate Speed steadily. Presently a smile touched the corners of her mouth.

"All right," she said. "Try to do it!"

Kate might have said more, probably would have done so, had not the train just then slowed down. They were nearing the station at Waterville.

Kate gave a little scream and rushed to her seat to gather luggage and wraps.

Lily Darrow followed patiently after, handing Kate her belongings before she ventured to look for her own.

"Of all the unpleasant people that Kate Speed is the worst!" fumed Nan, as the chums pulled their grips down from the rack.

"Sh!" warned Sadie. "She'll hear you."

"Hope she does!" grumbled Nan, though it might be noticed that she lowered her voice. "Wallop me, will she? I'll show her!"

Jo chuckled.

"Go to it, Nan! I'm crazy to see the first match between you and Speedy Kate!"

There was no time for further conversation as the train was already drawing in at the station.

In the excitement of leaving the train and embarking on the steamer that was to take them down the lake to Laurelton, the Woodford girls temporarily lost sight of Kate Speed and Lily Darrow.

"Though how Speedy Kate thinks we are going to find our way to Laurel Hall without her is a mystery," chuckled Sadie.

"To hear her talk you'd think we needed a governess," Nan agreed disgustedly. "I only hope I don't have to see a great deal of that girl. I don't know how much of her I could stand!"

With a crowd of other people the three girl chums bordered

the lake steamer and found comfortable places near the rail. From where they sat the beautiful waters of Twin Mountain Lake stretched invitingly before them. The sun, reflected in its rippling surface, shone dazzlingly. The irregular line of the shore, the numerous islands, black and mysterious, that bulked against the sparkling water seemed to beckon the girls on to new experiences, new adventures.

"We're off," cried Jo as the deck quivered beneath their feet with the throb of the engine. "If I'm dreaming, girls, please don't wake me up!"

There were several other girls of about their own age on the steamer, and the chums guessed that these were either students or, like themselves, prospective students of Laurel Hall.

Naturally these groups of young people interested the Woodford girls immensely, and the six-mile trip down the lake to Laurelton proved unexpectedly short.

Once they caught a glimpse of Kate Speed in a group of girls, talking animatedly. She never once glanced in their direction! But for this the chums were thankful.

"She seems to have fallen in with some old acquaintances. Naturally we are nothing to her now," said Nan, with a chuckle.

"She was peeved at the way you answered her tennis challenge," added Jo, laughing. "From the look on her face, I imagine you made a very dear enemy just then, Nan Harrison!"

"I'd a lot rather have some people for enemies than friends," retorted Nan.

When the steamer puffed up to the dock at Laurelton the girls disembarked like a group of chattering magpies.

For the most part they were nice-looking girls with eager, happy young faces that spoke of healthy minds and bodies, of good homes, and loving care.

"A pretty good crowd," Sadie whispered to Jo. "And they don't look at all like the sort Kate Speed said they were."

"We'll not take Kate Speed's word for anything," replied Jo. "I don't suppose she knows everything, even if she thinks she does."

Laurelton was an ordinary small country village with its main street, its few modest stores, and its unassuming cottages set well back from the street in ample grounds.

It was pretty in its way, but the girls were too intent upon "following the crowd" and finding the autobus to Laurel Hall to see much of the village on that first day.

There was a bus line that went straight past the gates of the school. Into one of the busses the girls crowded, the trio from Woodford feeling elatedly that they had at last embarked on the final stage of their journey.

The trunks and other luggage of the girls that had made the trip successfully with their owners were to remain in the custody of the boat company at the wharf until such time as the school truck should be dispatched for them.

It was a short ride from the village to Laurel Hall, almost too short for the three girl chums, who enjoyed every moment of the trip.

Kate Speed was in the rear seat of the bus with Lily Darrow and two other girls, who seemed to be very much of her own type.

There was a dark-haired girl in the seat next to Nan, and between Laurelton and Laurel Hall these two struck up quite a friendship.

The strange girl's name was Jessie Robinson, and she, like Kate Speed, had completed one year at Laurel Hall.

But there all resemblance ceased, for Jessie was a jolly, friendly girl who dressed in quiet good taste and appeared to be the exact opposite in every way of the flashy Kate Speed.

"Since you are new at the hall, I'd be glad to show you around if you like," she offered. "I know most of the girls and I can introduce you to some of them. It will sort of break the ice for you, anyway."

Nan promptly accepted the offer in the spirit in which it was made. She liked Jessie Robinson and found herself hoping that there were many more of her type at the Hall.

The auto bus swung round a curve in the road and revealed

to view two immense stone pillars between which a wrought iron gate was hung.

This gate now stood open, and as the horn of the bus blew a sharp warning several girls in bright-colored frocks ran through the entrance and down to the road.

"Laurel Hall!" cried Sadie in great excitement, and clutched at Jo's arm. "Look Jo—there it is standing up on the hill. Isn't it the most beautiful building in the world?"

"Looks like some sort of castle, with its turrets and towers and ivy-grown walls," Jo agreed.

"All out for Laurel Hall!" boomed the driver of the bus, and brought his vehicle to a stop at the side of the road.

The girls scrambled out, dragging bags and other small luggage after them.

Some were greeted by acquaintances who had arrived before them at the Hall. Others went directly toward the school building as though they already knew their way about; while still others, evidently new arrivals, looked about them vaguely as though they were at a loss just what to do next.

The three chums from Woodford would have been among this last group had not Jessie Robinson come to their rescue.

"Do you know what rooms you've been assigned to?" she asked, as she led them up the broad drive past chattering groups of girls toward the Hall.

"Not the least in the world," Jo answered for her chums.

"We asked for a large room with three single beds in it so that we could be together," Sadie added.

"But whether we get it or not is another matter!" finished Nan.

Jessie laughed.

"Well, of course you take what you get and feel yourself lucky enough to get anything, with the waiting list we have," she said. "Miss Jane is fair, though," she added. "She always tries to give the girls what they want and everybody loves her. Just wait till you see her and you won't wonder why!"

Jessie was besieged at the school steps by a flood of

acquaintances. She laughingly disengaged herself, however, and managed to reach the door of the Hall with her three new friends.

"Come up to my room later," she called back to the merry group. "We'll have a good pow-wow. I've loads to tell you."

Just inside the door was the office of Miss Jane Romaine, the head of Laurel Hall.

"There's Miss Jane now," whispered Jessie Robinson. "We'll have to go in and report, and then she'll tell you about your rooms."

The room was beautifully furnished with a heavy-pile rug, mahogany desk and chairs.

"It looks more like a sitting room than an office," Nan whispered to Jo. "Dad's office never looked like this!"

Jo nodded, but a sudden unhappy thought left its shadow on her face. Nan had reminded her of her own father and of his grave trouble.

However, Miss Jane Romaine looked up from her papers just then, and with a smile beckoned the girls closer.

"Well, Jessie," said the tall, thin lady with the beautiful dark eyes and white hair, "I am glad to welcome you back, my dear. I rather expected you among the girls who arrived yesterday."

"I was delayed a day by sickness at home," Jessie explained, and drew her new friends forward.

Miss Romaine's manner to the newcomers was cordial, friendly, simple. She asked their names, welcomed them both officially and personally to Laurel Hall and assigned them their rooms.

"Because you want to occupy a room together I have made a special concession in your favor," she told them with her pleasant smile. "I am going to give you the big north room overlooking the lake. It has an alcove, and you should be very comfortable there."

There was a stir in the rear of the room and a girl elbowed her way through a group of newcomers who were waiting to see Miss Romaine.

"The north room!" cried this girl, in a high, strident voice. "Why, they can't have that room! It belongs to me!"

CHAPTER XI

A VANQUISHED ENEMY

At the astonishing statement made by one of the schoolgirls, an excited murmur spread among the group gathered in the principal's office.

Miss Jane Romaine raised her fine brows and stared at the speaker.

"Nothing in Laurel Hall belongs to you or any other girl, Katherine," she said coldly, each word dropping like an icicle upon the surcharged atmosphere. "If you cannot enter this office in a becoming manner and wait to speak until you are spoken to, I am afraid I shall have to ask you to leave."

Kate Speed—for it was she—flushed angrily, started to speak, and then, at the last minute, thought better of it.

"Do I hear an apology?" Miss Romaine's tone was gentle, but underlying it was a ring of authority not to be denied.

"I'm—sorry," said Kate sullenly and as though she had to drag the words from between her unwilling lips. "But I thought— —"

"Stand a little back, Katherine, please." Miss Romaine's voice was suddenly crisp and business-like. "There are several girls who entered the office before you, and each one must take her turn."

She smiled at the three chums from Woodford, handed them each a printed slip upon which were detailed the rules of the school, gave them the number of their room, and waved them pleasantly away.

"I see you have already made a friend of Jessie. She will explain anything that puzzles you," she said, and added: "I hope you will be very happy at Laurel Hall."

On the way out of the office the girl chums were forced to pass close to Kate Speed and her little group of indignant associates. The fair-haired girl, who had recently professed such a friendly feeling for them, shot them a look of venomous dislike now that fairly startled them.

Once outside the door in the corridor, they all turned to Jessie Robinson. They were surprised to see that she was laughing silently but gleefully.

"Well, I must say I can't see where the joke comes in!" Jo, puzzled, exclaimed.

But Jessie tugged at her sleeve and drew the other girls after her up the broad staircase.

"Oh, come away, do!" she gasped. "I never saw anything so funny as Kate's face, never!"

"But she seemed mad at us," said Nan. "What was she angry about?"

"Wait till we get to your room and I'll explain," said Jessie, still breaking forth into irrepressible chuckles. "It's all simple enough once you know the facts. Here we are!"

As she spoke their new friend opened the door at the end of the hall and with a dramatic gesture motioned them to enter.

"Behold! This, once Kate Speed's domain, now belongs to you. Advance, conquerors, and take possession!"

"Oh, my goodness, I begin to see light!" cried Jo. "Do you mean to say this room was Kate's last year?"

"Even so," returned their new friend. She flung herself upon one of the single beds and, knees hugged comfortably beneath her chin, regarded them gleefully. "Now do you begin to see why our lovely Kate regards you with disfavor?"

"I suppose she wanted the same room this year," said Sadie, looking thoughtful.

"Then she should have said so—and said so early," retorted Jessie Robinson. "That's the way with Kate. She takes it for granted that she's so important that people ought to know what she wants without being told. She could have had this room if she'd asked for it early enough, but I suppose you girls got in your application first, and so Miss Jane turned it over to you. She plays no favorites, anyway."

"No wonder the girl wanted to murder us!" said Nan. "I can't say that I blame her much, now that I know the dreadful truth."

"This sure is one great room!" murmured Jo, and wandered over toward the window.

"Look, girls!" she called a moment later.

Nan and Sadie ran to her while Jessie Robinson continued to hug her knees and regard the chums with gleefully speculating eyes.

"The lake!" Jo gave a hop, skip, and jump of happy excitement. "If that isn't a million-dollar view, I'd like to know what is!"

"Ooh, we're right on it almost—the lake I mean, not the view!" cried Sadie. "I never saw anything so pretty as that water in all my life!"

"What have we done to deserve it?" chortled Nan. "Girls, this is the luck of a lifetime!"

A glance about the room and from the windows of it would fully explain the girls' delight in the quarters they were to occupy at Laurel Hall.

The room, besides being unusually large, boasted an alcove, as well, and three big windows. While in reality very simply furnished, the apartment had an air of comfort, almost of luxury, that was very inviting.

Each bed had an immaculate spread, and at the foot of each a comforter, folded diamond-shape, spoke of cool country nights when extra bed clothes were necessary to comfort.

Two of the beds were side by side in the main room, while the third occupied the alcove. This gave an effect of privacy, almost as though the alcove were another room.

There were three dressers, each one standing formal and upright against the wall. A table, some chairs, among them three big easy-chairs, and a small desk in the far corner completed the furnishings.

But if the room within was inviting, surely the view without was even more so.

From two of their three windows the lake could be seen, rippling placidly in the valley with the grim towering bulk of one of the twin mountains in the background looming black against a brilliant sky.

"Look! There's a dock!" cried Sadie. "I suppose that must belong to Laurel Hall."

"And there's our boathouse, too," Jessie Robinson came to look over their shoulders. "That's where we keep our bathing suits, oars, paddles, cushions, and such things. It's quite a sizable boathouse and it has lockers just like a gym."

"Makes me want to get out my bathing suit right now," said Nan longingly. "I wonder when our trunks will be up from Laurelton."

Suddenly Jo's brows contracted in a frown of concentration and she pointed with some excitement toward the boathouse.

"I wonder what's the matter!" she said. "Look at those girls down there running about like— —"

"Chickens with their heads cut off," Sadie finished. "Maybe there's a row or something."

"Might be worth investigating, anyway," said Jessie Robinson.

But as she turned from the window Nan caught her by the arm.

"They are coming this way. Maybe we can see from here."

"No, sir!" said their new friend sturdily. "When there's trouble brewing, little Jessie can always be found right in the middle of it. You wait here, if you like. I'm going down."

Of course the chums went with her, wondering about the excitement at the boathouse and what could have caused it.

They soon found themselves in a crowd of students surging eagerly to meet the party from the boathouse.

"Girls!" cried an advance envoy of the latter, "something dreadful has happened! The boathouse and the gym have both been broken into!"

It took a moment for the hearers to digest this astounding bit of news.

"You mean thieves?" some one cried.

"I'll say it was thieves!" cried several girls in chorus.

"Some of our swimming and gym suits have been taken!" cried another girl, her voice shrill above the din.

"And my tennis racket and a whole new set of balls!" wailed another.

"Doris Maybel, when did this happen?" Jessie Robinson elbowed her way into the throng. "Does Miss Jane know about it, yet?"

"I don't suppose so," said Doris, answering the last question first. "And it must have been last night that it happened, because some one has been about all day——"

"Girls!" The clear voice cut crisply across the excited babble of girls' voices. "What does this mean?"

CHAPTER XII

ROBBED

The students turned to find Miss Jane Romaine on the steps.

For a moment there was silence out of respect for the presence of the beloved head of Laurel Hall.

Then pandemonium broke loose again, the girls surging toward the slender, commanding figure on the steps.

Miss Romaine raised her hand and frowned slightly. Again silence fell, although some of the girls looked as though they would burst with the importance of the news they had to tell.

"Doris Maybel," Miss Romaine singled out the girl standing with Jessie Robinson, "suppose you tell me what the trouble is?"

Doris Maybel, short and blonde and very pretty, stepped forward quickly.

"Some of the girls and I thought we would like to try out the new apparatus we have in the gym, Miss Jane— —"

"Yes?" prompted Miss Romaine as the girl hesitated.

"Well, I guess nobody had been there before to-day. Anyway, there was nobody in the gym when we got there, but when we went to look for our gym suits we found that some of the lockers had been opened and some of the things in them taken. My own new gym suit was taken," she added, in conclusive proof of the robbery.

"And my new tennis racket and balls!" wailed another mourner from the crowd.

Miss Romaine raised her hand again, the furrows between her brows deepening.

"I suppose this must have happened last night," she said, then added sharply, turning to Doris: "Why was I not informed of this before?"

The girl started at the swift change of tone and hastened to justify herself.

"I came to tell you, Miss Jane," she said. "I asked for you everywhere, but no one seemed to know where you had gone. Then I came out here to look for you and met the other girls on their way from the boathouse."

"And some of the lockers were opened there, too, and things taken from them, Miss Jane!" broke in an excited girl in the crowd.

"My rowing suit is gone!" cried another.

Miss Romaine checked the growing confusion with a gesture of her hand.

"I will investigate this," she said. "And I want you, Doris, to go with me and show me what damage has been done. I have just one thing to say."

She paused and her large dark eyes swept the uplifted faces of the girls.

"This looks like the work of thieves. Since our head janitor, Mr. Forbes, has not yet arrived, robbers would have found it comparatively easy to break into the gym and the boathouse last night.

"I shall set an investigation afoot at once and if we find that this is an actual robbery we will do our utmost to apprehend and punish the thieves."

Again she paused and swept the girls with her slow, keen gaze.

"It has been our misfortune once or twice in the past," she said, speaking clearly, "to have harbored within the walls of Laurel Hall that worst of public nuisances, the practical joker. If I find," each word came clear and distinct like the tinkling of icicles upon stone, "that any one of my girls has been so unworthy as to play a trick of this sort, I warn her now that she may expect scant mercy from me. There is one thing that Laurel Hall cannot and will not tolerate—and that is the perpetrator of practical jokes."

She held them with the severity of her gaze for a moment

longer; then motioned to Doris and went with her toward the gymnasium.

The tension relaxed, and as soon as Miss Jane had disappeared, the girls broke up into chattering, excited, gesticulating groups.

Jessie Robinson was the center of one of these and seemed temporarily to have forgotten her new friends.

Feeling a bit out of things, the three chums decided to run up to their room—the room coveted by Kate Speed—to talk things over.

"Wherever I go these days, I seem to run into thieves," said Jo.

They had closed the door behind them and now exchanged rueful glances.

"First some one robs my father and just about ruins him," continued Jo, enlarging on her statement. "Then I come to Laurel Hall to find that some one has broken in here the night before I arrive. Guess I must be a jinx or something."

"A mighty nice jinx," said Nan affectionately.

She took off her hat, flung it on a bed, and sank into a chair with a prodigious yawn.

"Goodness, but I'm weary!"

"Who wouldn't be after the trip and now all this excitement." Sadie took off her coat and opened one of the closets in the room—there were two roomy ones. "Let's get our grips unpacked," she suggested. "The trunks ought to be up pretty soon, and we've got to get ready for dinner."

"I wonder who really did break into the gym," said Jo, frowningly concentrated on her own thoughts and seeming not to have heard Sadie.

Nan shook her head.

"Sounds more like a practical joke to me. Why should thieves want to break into a school gym and a boathouse? Wouldn't be enough in it for them."

"I don't know about that. Most of the girls' things were

brand new and probably could be sold again at a fairly good price."

"I still think it's a practical joke," insisted Nan. She rose lazily and went over to one of the dresser mirrors where she critically inspected her reflection. "Dear me, look at that streak of dirt across my nose! I look a sight!"

"I don't think it's a practical joke." Jo could not be shaken from the subject. "A girl might open one locker just to be funny. But she wouldn't be apt to go about opening them wholesale. That would be silly, because it would only get her into heaps of trouble."

"It probably will—if Miss Jane finds her out." Nan was as persistent in her theory as Jo was in hers. "I certainly would hate to be that girl!"

There was the sound of footsteps and laughter in the hall outside.

The next moment the door burst open and three girls entered the room. One was Jessie Robinson, another Doris Maybel. The third was as yet unknown to the chums.

"Here's a fine row," said Jessie without preface. "Miss Jane is bound to find the girl or girls who played that practical joke, and there isn't a girl in the school but what suspects every other girl of being the guilty one. A fine time we're going to have at Laurel Hall for the next few days, I can see that!"

At this point the impulsive girl appeared to realize that new friends and old had not, as yet, been properly introduced and promptly set herself to correct the error.

"This is Doris Maybel," she said. "We room together, although our room isn't anywhere near as nice as this. And this," thrusting forward the third of the trio, "is Gladys Holt—a nice girl if you don't cross her——"

"Then she's cross," said Doris, and they all laughed together at the feeble joke.

"Now listen, girls, don't give me a bad reputation at the start," drawled Gladys, as she perched herself on the rail of the bed and regarded the party with twinkling eyes. "No telling how I may end up, but I want to get off on the right foot, anyway!"

"Jessie has told us how mad Kate Speed is that you have her room," Doris flung herself into a chair near the chums and pushed back the hair from her warm face. She was smiling as though in anticipation of a joyful prospect. "We expect to get a lot of fun out of this, let me tell you."

"Believe me, we will!" chuckled Jessie. "I happened to pass Kate's room a few minutes ago," she added. "The door was open, and I looked in."

"What kind of a room was it?" Jo interrupted with interest.

"Oh, not so bad——"

"And not so good," supplemented Gladys. "I happen to know that room, and I can tell you it's cold in winter!"

"Well, anyway, it has an alcove something like this," Jessie explained, with a wave of her hand. "It's a 'three girls' room,' anyway, and that's what Kate wants. But of course it's smaller than this one and it has only two windows. Kate was furious. She was railing at poor Lily Darrow as if it was all her fault, though how it could be, goodness only knows."

"And I suppose Lily was sitting with her hands crossed and taking it all meekly," Doris interrupted, with an impatient bounce in her chair. "Sometimes I lose all patience with that girl. I don't believe she has any spine!"

"We met them both on the train coming up," Sadie offered.

"And it seemed to us as if Lily Darrow was afraid to own her own name," Jo added.

Their three new friends nodded solemnly and Jessie pounded one small brown fist in the other by way of emphasis.

"There's something funny about the friendship between those two," she said. "I guess every girl in the school has tried to get Lily Darrow away from Kate at some time or other——"

"We all feel sorry for Lily—she has such a frightful time of it," Doris said, in an aside.

"But she won't budge," Jessie finished. "She hates Kate——"

"Any one could see that with half an eye!" drawled Gladys Holt.

"And she's mortally afraid of her, and yet she sticks to her like a fly to flypaper," finished Jessie. "We can't understand it, and it makes us mad."

"Is Lily Darrow the only close friend Kate has?" asked Jo, who had listened to all this with great interest.

"Oh, my goodness, no!"

The three visitors exchanged laughing glances and Jessie chuckled audibly.

"Kate has what Miss Slade, our dramatics teacher, calls an 'understudy,'" Jessie explained. "Lottie Sparks is her shadow. She thinks Kate is grand because she has a lot of money, and she does exactly what Kate tells her to do."

"In other words," said Gladys Holt, lazily stretching her arms above her head, "Kate makes the bombs and Lottie fires them."

"That's just it!" cried Jessie. "Whatever Lottie says, you can be pretty sure that Kate prompted her ahead of time."

"Lottie's noisy, but Kate's sly," offered Doris.

"Those two girls have made more trouble at Laurel Hall than all the rest put together," Jessie said energetically.

"Oh, well," laughed Doris, "let's forget about Kate and Lottie for a while. I can think of lots pleasanter things to talk about."

As she finished speaking, as though to put a period to her sentence, a loud gong rang sonorously through the halls.

The visiting girls sprang to their feet.

"The preliminary gong," explained Jessie. "Just fifteen minutes to get ready for supper. Excuse us while we rush!"

"Hey, wait a minute!" Jo caught one of the girls as she flew past and held on to her. "Which way is the dining hall?"

"We'll call for you," Jessie promised. "See you later!" The door slammed shut.

CHAPTER XIII

THE ENGLISH TEACHER

"Aren't they awfully nice?" cried Sadie, as the three girl chums rushed about in a flurried effort to make themselves presentable for their first meal at Laurel Hall.

"Lovely! But for goodness' sake, which one of you girls has my brush and comb?" This from Nan as she looked frantically for something with which to smooth her ruffled fair hair.

"I'd suggest you look in your grip," said Jo dryly, and received a gloomy stare from her best friend.

"Idiot! Do you think I haven't?"

"Here it is." Sadie came pacifically into the breach, handing Nan her lost articles.

"Where did you get 'em?" grumbled Nan, in no mood to be pacified.

"On the bed, where you put them yourself," retorted Sadie. "You don't think I opened your old grip, do you?"

"Stop fighting!" This came from Jo as she dipped her face into a basin of clear cold water and came up sputtering and rosy. "We have about two minutes to get ready."

Thanks to the sociability of their new friends, they had no time to change their dresses. But whisk brooms were brought forth, collars and belts smoothed into place, and shoes rubbed with a cloth for want of time to polish them.

This concession to respectability together with freshly washed faces and smooth, shining hair wrought a pleasing change in the girls. When the supper gong rang they looked as well groomed as though they had just been freshly tubbed and had had a change of clothes from head to foot.

Jessie Robinson was true to her promise and appeared at their door just as the supper gong rang.

"Doris and Gladys are still primping," she explained, out of breath with haste. "Miss Jane can't bear tardiness, so I told them I'd come on without them. Are you ready?"

"All ready," said Jo, and added with exasperation: "Except Sade, who seems to have gone back to the wash basin!"

"I found a smudge on the side of my nose," Sadie explained, rubbing the offending spot vigorously as she hurried toward them. "Is it off now?" anxiously.

"If it isn't, it won't be," replied Jo. "Come on!"

But Nan added reassuringly.

"All O. K., Sadie dear. You're as fresh as the flowers in June—or is it May?"

Jessie led them through the hall and down the broad flight of stairs that they had already twice ascended. They met other groups of girls and mingled with them in a happy spirit of comradeship.

"Our first meal at Laurel Hall!" Sadie surreptitiously squeezed Jo's hand as they neared a large door through which floated appetizing odors. "Isn't it scrumptious?"

Jo only smiled in answer, for they had reached the dining hall.

"There's Miss Tully—the teacher in charge this week," Jessie said. "She will assign you your places at table."

The three Woodford girls regarded Miss Tully with interest, as being the first of the faculty, with the exception of Miss Romaine, whom they had yet seen.

Miss Tully was of medium height. She was very thin, almost, the new girls thought, the thinnest person they had ever seen. She wore her hair drawn severely back from a severe brow and her gray eyes, small and bright under level brows, carried out this general impression of severity.

All in all, from the moment of looking at Miss Tully the three chums found themselves in awe of her and avoided the glance of that hard gray eye with dexterity. Miss Tully, while being an excellent disciplinarian, was not popular with the girls of Laurel Hall nor with the rest of the faculty.

"Gracious, I hope they're not all like her!" whispered Nan Harrison irrepressibly, and was treated to a nudge by Jo.

"Keep still!" she whispered back. "Do you want her to put you in the dungeon?"

Miss Tully was indeed glancing in their direction with a contraction of her heavy brows that might have been disapproval. In this case it was merely mental concentration, but the girls could not have been expected to know that.

"Your names, young ladies?" asked the teacher, as Jessie drew her new friends forward.

The girls introduced themselves and were relieved when that frown of concentration turned from them to a slip Miss Tully held in her hand.

"You are at the third table," she told them finally. "Third, fourth, and fifth seats from the foot. Show them their places, Jessie, if you please," and she turned her attention to the next group of new girls entering the room.

"Glory! You're at my table!" whispered Jessie, as she piloted the girls down the long room. "And, even better than that, your seats are right next to Doris and me!"

This was a very happy arrangement for the chums. They felt that, instead of living for a certain period of time among strange girls with whom they would have to become acquainted by degrees, they had fallen into the hands of friends.

"You are making it mighty nice for us," Jo whispered, and Jessie answered only with a bright smile.

The dining hall was a long narrow room with windows along one entire side of it. Since the chums knew that Laurel Hall accommodated at the least eighty students and at the most ninety, they were prepared for the thought that the dining hall must be of a considerable size to seat them all at meals.

Long, tables furnished the room, and at these almost all the girls of Laurel Hall were already assembled.

Table three proved to be at the foot of the long room, but near the cheerful bright stretch of windows. From these windows the view was beautiful and even included a small portion of the lake.

The pleasure of the chums at being placed close to their new friends was tempered by a discovery they made as they drew their chairs out from the table. Directly opposite them, sat Kate Speed and her meek little shadow, Lily Darrow!

"I had no idea that you were to sit at our table or I might have warned you," Jessie whispered, noting Jo's glance of annoyance. "Never mind, Kate can't bite at meals. Not with Miss Tully in charge!"

Kate Speed, who had been talking across a vacant place to a girl on her side of the table, happened to look up at this moment.

She stared at the three girls who—most innocently—occupied the room she coveted. She then caught the laughing, teasing gaze of Jessie Robinson.

Kate stiffened and tossed her head with an air of haughty disdain. Without deigning to recognize the presence of the girls with whom she had been so effusively friendly on the train, she turned and began an ostentatious conversation with quiet Lily Darrow.

Jo nudged Nan, who was sitting next to her.

"Cut—by cricky!" she chuckled, and then exchanged laughing glances with Sadie, on the other side of Nan.

Meanwhile Jessie was glancing nervously over her shoulder. The two vacant seats at the foot of the table belonged to Doris Maybel and Gladys Holt. Neither of the girls had come in yet, although Miss Tully had assigned the last new girl her seat and was about to take her own place at the head of table one.

"I feel sorry for them if they're late," whispered Jessie in response to Jo's question. "They ought to know better—with Tully in charge!"

At the moment there was a stir at the door and Jessie looked hopeful. But it was only Miss Jane Romaine, come to have a word with the teacher in charge.

Jessie's foot began to tap the floor—tap—tap—under the edge of the table.

"There they are!" cried Nan suddenly, as two guilty heads poked in at the door.

CHAPTER XIV

A MEAN TRICK

If the teacher in charge had not been so deeply engrossed in conversation with Miss Romaine, Doris Maybel and Gladys Holt could never have reached their places at table without detection and subsequent reproof for tardiness.

As it was, they were very nearly caught. The culprits afterward declared with a good deal of indignation that it was certainly not Kate Speed's fault that they were not, for at the moment when, having slipped as silently as ghosts down the long room, they pulled back their chairs at table, thinking to have reached their goal at last and in safety, Kate Speed gave a loud cough that instantly attracted Miss Tully's attention to table three.

If the teacher had been alone neither girl could have escaped her keen gray eyes.

But Miss Romaine instantly claimed her attention again and the culprits sank thankfully into their places.

Across the table their glances challenged Kate Speed angrily. Others were looking at Kate, a disgusted question in their eyes.

Lily Darrow, her face red, sat with eyes fixed on her plate.

Kate Speed met the unfriendly glances turned in her direction with a toss of her head and a faint, disdainful smile on her lips.

"People who are late deserve to be shown up," she was heard to say in a loud stage whisper to Lily Darrow.

Doris Maybel seemed about to fling a wrathful reply across the table, but a vigorous stamp of Jessie's foot on hers beneath the table warned her to be cautious.

Miss Tully, in the act of seating herself at the table, glanced in their direction.

Silence fell upon table three and each girl stared innocently platewards.

Miss Tully took her seat and, though the teacher's back was still very rigid, the rest of the room seemed to relax. As the soup was brought in, conversation recommenced, a low-toned and guarded conversation, to be sure—for though the girls were encouraged to talk at meals, no loud laughter or conversation was allowed—at any rate, not with Miss Tully presiding over the room.

Nan and Sadie and Jo set to with a will upon the tempting dishes. They had not tasted food since the rather early lunch on the train, and they were very hungry.

"I only wish we had come to Laurel Hall in time for dinner instead of supper," Nan said in a low tone to Sadie. "I could do with a six course meal right now."

"This looks pretty good to me," returned Sadie, as the empty soup dishes were removed and platters of cold meat were passed around the table, along with tea biscuits.

A generous plate of egg salad was put at each girl's place with a glass of rich creamy milk. For dessert there was layer cake and homemade cookies and cup custard.

"We won't starve to death, that's one sure thing," said Jo, as she helped herself for the second time to meat and looked hungrily at the egg salad.

After dinner the chums wandered out into the beautiful grounds of Laurel Hall. Their new friends went with them, to "show them the sights."

"Though we can't stay out very long," Jessie said regretfully. "The rule is, every one in rooms by eight o'clock, lights out by nine. And with winter coming on and the days getting so short we hardly have any time at all after supper."

To the three Woodford girls the grounds about Laurel Hall were even more beautiful than they had imagined them.

The Hall was set in the midst of a considerable property. There were not many trees, for a great number of these had been sacrificed for the sake of the lawn that stretched like a piece of green velvet from the road almost to the borders of the lake. What trees there were were grand old patriarchs, tremendous in girth, heavy branches sweeping upward toward the sky.

About three of these beautiful old trees rustic benches had been fashioned, and these seats were almost always occupied by groups of laughing girls.

The shadows were falling thickly as a number of the girls made their way down to the boathouse on the shores of the lake. The water was only a shimmer of gray against a darker background.

The towering mountain that had seemed only picturesque in the brilliant glare of the afternoon sun now rose dark and mysterious against the shadowy sky.

Sight of the boathouse reminded the girls of the mysterious happenings connected with it.

"We aren't going inside, are we?" asked Sadie a shade nervously.

Doris Maybel laughed.

"Not a chance! It's strictly against the rules to enter the boathouse after dark."

Jo chuckled.

"For once we can enjoy obeying a rule!" she said.

As the Woodford chums and their new friends came nearer to the boathouse that loomed like a dark blot against the landscape, they were astonished and a bit startled to hear voices.

The fact that they were voices was little. The fact that they were men's voices was much.

The girls paused and looked at each other, uncertain whether to advance or retreat. Curiosity urged them on. Caution advised retreat.

"The thieves!" murmured Sadie uneasily. "I think we'd better get out of here!"

But Jo caught her arm.

"Wait a minute!" she cried. "Listen!"

CHAPTER XV

IN THE DUSK

The girls had crept closer and were near enough to hear what the men said.

The latter seemed to be on the far side of the boathouse. They had evidently neither seen nor heard the girls.

"I tell you, Jim, it was a slick job," came the low, gruff voice of one of the men.

"They are the thieves!" whispered Sadie, and tugged at the arm that was still in Jo's grasp.

"Oh, hush!" cried the latter. "Listen!"

"It sure was," responded a second voice, lighter in timbre and less guarded, as though the speaker were a younger man than his companion. "It was so well done that Miss Romaine thinks it the work of some mischievous girls."

Both men laughed and the girls looked at each other inquiringly.

"That voice doesn't sound like a thief's voice to me," remarked Nan.

"Listen!" cried Jo again.

"The crooks are slick ones and they're probably responsible for some other small robberies in town," came the voice of the first speaker. "But we'll find 'em yet, you bet!"

"Sure—with Old Hawkeye on the job!" responded the younger voice in a chaffing way. "Well, we might as well go up to the Hall and report on what we've found."

"You mean what we haven't found!" retorted the other voice disgustedly.

The girls shrank back against the boathouse as two shadows detached themselves from the farther side of it and went off in the direction of the Hall.

Jessie began to giggle, and her merriment was contagious.

"Of all the idiots, we are the worst!" laughed Jo. "They are detectives or policemen or something or other on that order, and we took them for burglars!"

"That was the sheriff from Laurelton and his helper," Gladys explained. "My father knows the sheriff. His name is Ebenezer Crabb and Dad told me once he's so stupid he wouldn't know a crook if he saw one."

"That looks fine for our chance of catching the thieves," remarked Sadie, as they started toward the Hall again.

"Meanwhile everybody in the school is suspected of playing practical jokes," said Doris with a discontented shrug of her shoulders. "I declare, I'm beginning to feel guilty about it myself!"

"Anyway, there's one bit of luck for us," remarked Nan. "And that is that we didn't get here until after the robbery was committed."

"Yes," said Jo, looking very innocent. "We, at least, are above suspicion!"

Tired as they were, the three chums were so fascinated with their new surroundings and their new friends that the preliminary bell for "all lights out" found them still unwilling to go to their room.

"To-morrow's Sunday so we shall be expected to go to church in the morning," said Jessie, as they lingered in the hall for a last word. "But in the afternoon after dinner we'll show you all about the place."

"I want to see the tennis courts. Don't forget the tennis courts," begged Nan.

"We won't forget the tennis courts," their new friends laughed, and with a last gay wave of the hand went off toward their own rooms.

The three girl chums were so full of the crowding experience of the day that they had expected to stay up for the best part of the night—surreptitiously of course and ready to jump into bed at the first sound in the corridor—discussing them.

But they had counted without the comfortable beds at Laurel Hall and their own complete exhaustion. Three heads had scarcely touched three pillows before three pairs of eyes closed in dreamless sleep.

That was the end of the first day at Laurel Hall.

After that several days flew by in rapid succession, each so crowded with pleasant experiences that the girls scarcely noticed their going.

Long letters were written home, fairly bulging with news. Jo started something which interested Sadie and was heartily approved by Nan. This was a diary—or, as Jo preferred to call it, a journal in which she recorded daily the most interesting doings of that day. Jo could write amusingly. Her wit always sparkled more on paper than in speech. The journal that she prepared for that first week was so funny when read aloud to a roomful of girls that she was unanimously acclaimed a "coming literary light."

"We have been harboring a genius in our midst," Gladys Holt declaimed with full dramatic effect. "I'm going to speak to Gerry Middleton about you, and if she doesn't get you a job on the Pied Piper she hasn't as much sense as they give her credit for."

Jo giggled, but looked pleased just the same. Geraldine—familiarly known as Gerry—Middleton was editor-in-chief of the school paper, Pied Piper. Besides holding this exalted position, Gerry was a senior and one of the most popular girls at Laurel Hall.

"I don't believe I could write like this for the public eye—" Jo said modestly.

"The vulgar public," interposed Nan.

"Anyway, this is strictly for private consumption," finished Jo, gayly tapping the journal on the fluffy head of Doris who was sitting directly beneath her on nothing more comfortable than the floor. "I wrote it to cheer up an invalid." She looked over intervening heads until her eye met Nan's. "It's for your Aunt Emma, Nan. I thought she might like it."

"Say, Jo, that's a bully scheme!" Nan was radiant. "It will be the best tonic in the world for her!"

So it happened that the new friends of the chums from Woodford came to hear about Nan's invalid aunt. Being kind-hearted girls, they took a genuine interest in the unfortunate woman. And, knowing of Jo's "journal," they saved up scraps of interesting or funny happenings of the day and brought them to lay in the lap of the "literary light."

Miss Emma wrote back cheerfully and affectionately, and her genuine and enthusiastic appreciation of the journal spurred Jo on to fresh efforts.

Meanwhile, the girl chums were becoming well accustomed to the pleasant routine of classes and recreation at Laurel Hall. On Sundays most of the girls put on their best frocks and went in automobiles to Laurelton and church.

This was both pleasant and sad to Jo, who thought more of her parents' troubles on Sundays than on other days—perhaps because then she had more time to think.

She gathered from her mother's letters—which arrived far more regularly and voluminously than the brief and hastily scrawled missives of her father—that nothing had as yet been heard of Andrew Simmer.

> "Your father is striving frantically to save something from the wreck," wrote Mrs. Morley. "If anybody could do it, he will, you may be sure, for his energy and courage are remarkable. He is a father to be proud of, Jo, but I sometimes wonder if his health will bear the strain."

Portions like this from her mother's letters repeated themselves over and over again while Jo attended church. She would be overwhelmed with a great melancholy and accuse herself, illogically enough, for having deserted her parents in their hour of need.

"It is wicked of me to be living here at Laurel Hall, surrounded by all sorts of comforts, luxuries, almost, while they are struggling at home. I'm going home! I'm going home to-morrow!"

But with to-morrow would come a saner mood, Jo realizing that she would only increase the worries of those at home by yielding to her impulse. She could help them more by staying where she was.

The members of the faculty at Laurel Hall were almost all liked by the girls. If there was an exception to this rule it was Miss Tully, the English teacher. It was rumored that Miss Tully was a snob, that she favored Kate Speed and Kate's chum Lottie Sparks because they were by far the richest girls in Laurel Hall.

"Anyway, she listens to everything those girls say when they come running with tales about the others," Doris Maybel said, with a shake of her curly head. "And if you notice, she generally decides in their favor. You just watch out and see if it isn't so!"

It was not long before the girls had an opportunity to test the truth of this statement.

By the end of the first week at Laurel Hall the three chums were well established in classes. They enjoyed their studies and liked their teachers—with that one exception.

Laurel Hall had been built originally by a wealthy Englishman. In this summer home he had copied as closely as possible the architecture of feudal England. Except that it was built of wood instead of stone, Laurel Hall might have been a miniature castle out of a story book.

Having built this ostentatious home for himself, the Englishman was called back to his native country and was forced to sell his property at a sacrifice. Miss Romaine, looking for just such a place at the time, had unhesitatingly closed the deal that was most satisfactory to both parties.

Of course all this had happened years before the three

chums were ready for school, but Laurel Hall remained substantially as it was when the sale took place.

One entered a great square hall from which a broad stairway ascended to a gallery above. Numerous rooms opened from this gallery and formed the dormitories of the students. There was a third floor, but only a few rooms were finished off here, and they were mostly occupied by servants. There was a great open attic also, and from this ran tiny fascinating stairways—scarcely more than ladders—ascending into turrets, and tower rooms from which one could gain a view of the countryside.

On the first floor were the classrooms, a large drawing, and a reception room, the dining hall already described and the rooms occupied by members of the faculty. The kitchen, presided over by a Negro cook named Nora, had been built on later and never seemed quite in keeping with the rest of the place. The girls liked it, however, as Nora often slipped them handfuls of fresh cookies out of the side door and never objected to making up picnic lunches whenever they were required. The kitchen was, the students thought, the pleasantest and most homelike place at Laurel Hall.

Now, for the members of the faculty.

Miss Travers, the teacher of mathematics, a slight energetic woman with an intellectual face, was well on in her fifties, yet carried with her a heart that was eternally young and in complete sympathy with the moods and caprices of her young charges.

The girls loved her, and, in lieu of mother just then, came to her with their troubles and problems, always sure of complete understanding and kindly guidance.

While the girls had a great affection for Miss Romaine, who was always pleasant and gracious and rigidly just, they could not approach her as they did Miss Travers, for she seemed to stand aloof from them surrounded by the wall of her reserve.

Then there was absent-minded Miss Ridley, the teacher of history. Except when teaching this subject dear to her heart, Miss

Ridley seemed to dwell on a strange and infinitely remote planet all her own. She could never remember names, and the girls soon learned that a culprit coming unprepared to one of Miss Ridley's classes, could, by gazing always demurely at her desk, avoid detection.

For Miss Ridley when she asked a question would invariably point at any one who happened to be looking in her direction and snap out crisply, "You tell me!"

Those that did not look in Miss Ridley's direction were seldom called upon for recitation, since that lady was loath to admit that she could not remember names.

"Another good way is to get her started talking history," one of these knowing young ones giggled after a particularly absent-minded session with Miss Ridley. "She'll talk the period through and forget at the end of it that she has not called on a single person for recitation!"

Nevertheless, the girls learned history in Miss Ridley's class. Perhaps it was because the teacher herself was so passionately interested in the subject that she got her enthusiasm across to her students. At any rate, her lectures, always started by some innocent, demure-looking girl with a guilty secret up her sleeve, were more informative and created a more lasting impression than any amount of class recitation could have done.

There were the teachers of languages too—Miss Drew whom, the girls declared, thought and prayed in Latin and Greek and dwelt in spirit among the early Hellenes, who never tired of telling the girls about Pelasgic Greece and the marvelous Tyrinthian wall.

"Imagine a wall fifty feet high and thirty feet thick!" interpolated a wide-eyed girl with an irreverent giggle. "Imagine having to scale that to get out to a party!"

There was the sweet-faced French teacher, a widow by the name of Briais, and Miss Handel, the portly German instructress. The music teacher, Miss Blitz, who wore her hair in a wild bob and was really an exceptional performer on the piano, provided a great deal of innocent amusement for her pupils.

The most youthful of all the members of the faculty at Laurel Hall was Miss Talley, physical culture teacher. She was fresh from college, hardly more than a girl, and she led her pupils through gymnastic performances at a stiff pace that they sometimes found rather hard to match.

They liked her youth and energy, however, and the fact that she encouraged athletics.

It was Miss Talley who watched the girls at tennis and gave them points—she played a smashing game herself. It was Miss Talley who arranged swimming and rowing races among the girls of the different grades and herself was always ready to out-row or out-swim the best of them.

It was on the tennis courts that the girls from Woodford had their first run-in with Kate Speed's crony, the snappy Lottie Sparks.

"I'll say that girl fits her name," Nan had remarked after meeting Lottie on that first Monday of the opening of school. "Lottie Sparks! It ought to be 'Lottie Spitfire.' I bet that girl goes off like a load of dynamite at the slightest provocation."

The words proved prophetic. A few days later the chums were given a sample of Lottie Sparks' temper that they did not very easily forget.

It happened on the tennis courts. For three days there had been a maddening drizzle of rain, making the courts too wet for tennis practice. The lake, too, was uninviting, and Jo and Sadie, eager to try some work at the oars, gave up all thought of boating until the weather should take a turn for the better.

At last on the fourth day the sun came out, feebly, to be sure, but welcomed joyfully by the watching girls.

After lessons they ran pellmell for the gymnasium where their rackets and balls were kept in individual lockers.

"The court will be pretty wet," Nan said, as she drew her racket from its case.

"We may need skid chains," Sadie agreed, with a chuckle. "But who cares? We can bat the ball about a bit, anyway."

The three chums of Woodford were the first to reach the wet and slippery tennis courts.

Sadie was joyfully trying out her rather uncertain service against Nan's smashing backhand when Kate Speed and Lottie Sparks came along, school books in hand.

They stopped to watch the practice, and perhaps it was this unfriendly inspection that flustered Sadie.

At any rate, she sent the ball spinning across the net in a ludicrously wild serve. It bounded from the muddy ground and caught Lottie Sparks squarely on the ear!

"Oh, my goodness!" cried Sadie, in consternation. "Now, what have I done?"

CHAPTER XVI

A MUDDY TENNIS BALL

Nan and Jo ran to join Sadie in an instinctive gesture of defense.

Lottie Sparks staggered beneath the blow—for it was really a pretty hard wallop—but rallied the next moment in admirable style.

She wiped the mud from her ear as several of the other girls, sensing a scene, came running up. A flush of fury spread over Lottie's dark face. She had been made ridiculous. Out of the corner of her eye she could see that some of the girls were trying to hide their amusement at sight of her mud-streaked face. Others were tittering outright.

"Of all the outrageous things!" cried Kate Speed, adding fuel to her crony's wrath. "You might know one of those Woodford girls would try a thing like that!"

"I don't know what you mean, Kate Speed!" cried Jo, stepping forward angrily.

Nan spoke urgently to her more fiery chum.

"Don't make a scene, Jo. Let it go." Then to Sadie, "Tell the girl you're sorry, Sade. We don't want any trouble."

Sadie, who had been too dismayed and conscience-stricken to attempt any explanation now stepped forward, stammering some sort of apology.

"I'm sorry," she said. "I didn't mean——"

"Oh, you're sorry, are you?" Lottie Sparks caught her up viciously, enraged at the more audible titters of the girls near her. "You didn't mean it, didn't you? Oh, no, of course you didn't! Your kind is always innocent! But don't think you can fool me. You did it on purpose!"

At this totally unjust accusation the usually gentle Sadie became roused to fighting pitch.

"I did not!" she cried, and took another step forward. "Don't dare say such a thing, you——"

The words died in mid-air. A long sigh of consternation rose from the watching girls.

Lottie Sparks, beside herself with rage, took careful aim, and, with all her might, threw one of her school books straight at Sadie's head!

Lucky for Sadie that she saw the missile coming and dodged!

The heavy book whizzed past her ear and came to rest in the muddy ground of the tennis court.

This was too much!

Sadie, with Nan and Jo to back her up, advanced upon her belligerent enemy.

There was a murmur of excitement among the girls. They crowded closer to watch what promised to be a battle royal.

There is no telling what might have come of the argument had not the English teacher appeared at that moment.

"Girls! Girls!" Miss Tully cried in her crisp, precise voice. "Pray, what is the meaning of this? What has happened?"

Kate Speed got in her innings first.

"It was all Sadie Appleby's fault, Miss Tully!" she cried. "She threw a muddy tennis ball at Lottie and hit her in the ear."

"I did not, Miss Tully," cried Sadie hotly. "I never thought of such a thing. It was an accident and I've already told Lottie Sparks I'm sorry."

"She threw it at me, Miss Tully," Lottie insisted. "She did it just to be mean!"

"Oh, she did not! That's a falsehood!" Jo cried out. Miss Tully turned sharply upon her.

"What kind of language is this for a student of Laurel Hall?" she reproved, looking sternly at the open-mouthed Jo. "Miss Josephine Morley, you will do better in the future to set a guard upon your tongue."

Lottie Sparks was beginning to look triumphant. Kate Speed tossed her fair head insolently. "I told you so!" was written plainly over the faces of both of them.

Jo's face burned red with an angry sense of injustice. Nan and Sadie were equally amazed and impotent.

Jo made one last attempt.

"But, Miss Tully——"

"That will do!" Miss Tully's acidulous tone put a definite end to the controversy. "I will set the facts of this disgusting quarrel before Miss Romaine and she will decide upon the sort of punishment to be meted out to the culprit. It is a disgrace to Laurel Hall that such a scene could occur within its grounds."

Her stern gaze traveled over the three chums from Woodford.

"I am here now, Miss Tully," came a clear, calm voice from behind the English teacher. "May I ask what all this trouble is about?"

With relief, Sadie, Jo, and Nan turned toward Miss Romaine as she made her way into the center of the group. Miss Romaine was fair. She would not judge without a hearing!

Miss Tully lost some of her assurance at sight of her superior. Lottie and Kate also lost their self-satisfied smiles and began to look anxious.

Questioned by Miss Romaine, the English teacher gave the details of both sides of the quarrel as she had heard them.

"I was about to lay the facts before you and let you decide as you thought fit," Miss Tully finished stiffly.

"Quite right," said Miss Romaine, who was always careful to uphold her teachers before the girls, however she might disagree with them in private. Then she turned gravely to Sadie Appleby.

"Then you say again that this was an accident and that you have already apologized to Lottie?" she asked.

Sadie nodded.

"I certainly do, Miss Jane," she said in all earnestness.

Lottie started forward.

"Miss Jane, she did it just to be mean. She did it on purpose!"

Miss Romaine turned swiftly upon the girl.

"That is ridiculous, Lottie Sparks, and I am ashamed that a girl of mine could make such an accusation. Sadie has said that it was an accident and has apologized. You must accept her apology and forget the incident. I will not hear another word on the subject!"

Miss Romaine turned away, frowning. Thoroughly cowed, but smoldering with resentment, Lottie Sparks stepped back to let her pass.

Miss Tully had already slipped away, and as the chums from Woodford turned back to the tennis courts they saw the English teacher entering the Hall.

Jo could not avoid crowing a little over the vanquished enemy.

She picked up Lottie Sparks' book and, with a twinkle in her eye, handed it to the owner.

"You may need it again some time," she said.

Lottie Sparks snatched at the book.

"Maybe I will," she said, and added vindictively: "Next time I won't miss with it, either!"

This was the first declaration of open warfare between the two camps. But scarcely a day passed after the incident of the tennis courts that either Kate or her friend did not find some excuse for annoying or slighting the chums from Woodford.

The girls could afford to laugh at most of these annoyances. They were popular with the rest of their classmates—with all, that is, who did not comprise Kate Speed's snobbish following—and they were content to give those unpleasant girls a wide berth.

Then one day toward the end of their third week at Laurel Hall, there came more startling news.

Thieves had been at work again the night before, only that this time they had done their task more thoroughly.

About five o'clock in the morning the janitor, who slept in a room over the garage that was used for Miss Romaine's sedan and a Ford truck which carried supplies from the village to the

Hall, was awakened by the put-putting of a motor boat on the lake. He saw two men set off in it, apparently leaving the Laurel Hall dock.

With the first robbery in mind and feeling uneasy, the janitor dressed quickly and made the rounds of the gymnasium and the boathouse. Here he found his suspicions justified. The gymnasium and the boathouse had both been robbed again!

The janitor went directly to Miss Romaine with his report. In some way the news leaked out before the Head of Laurel Hall intended it should. Like wildfire it spread among the excited girls.

"The lockers in the gym have been practically cleaned out!" wailed Nan.

"We should have slept with our things under our beds, that's what we should have done!" cried Sadie.

"I don't want to sleep under a bed!" Nan said crossly. "I prefer a mattress."

"I was speaking of the things, silly, not ourselves," retorted Sadie, with withering scorn.

Nan got up and walked restlessly about the room. In the course of her rambles her eye happened to light upon three tennis rackets, carefully cased and standing each in its own place against the wall.

"Anyway, we've some luck," she said, brightening. "We've managed to save our rackets out of the wreck."

"Yes, but how about my gym suit?" said Jo gloomily. "Chances are I'll not get another."

"Cheer up! Maybe some of the stuff will be found," said Sadie optimistically.

"Not with that long-whiskered sheriff down in the village and his short-brained helper on the job," said Nan flippantly. "If they didn't catch the thieves before, there's not much chance of their doing it now. A fine mess we're in, I'll say!"

That afternoon Miss Romaine called a special meeting of all the students of Laurel Hall in the auditorium.

She spoke simply and sincerely of the second robbery,

sympathizing with the girls who had lost their property and assuring them that no effort would be spared to apprehend the thieves and recover the stolen articles.

But in spite of these assurances the girls remained uneasy and nervous.

"How do we know that this thief isn't some sort of maniac?" one of them suggested.

"It certainly sounds like the work of a crazy man," another admitted.

This dread supposition spread through the school like fire and for days after the second robbery scarcely a girl could be found who would set foot in the grounds of Laurel Hall after dark.

The local police, represented by the sheriff and his assistant, were being stirred to real effort by the insistence of Miss Romaine and the girls hoped daily that they would receive some word in regard to their stolen property and the identity of the thieves.

Poor Jo was in a worse plight than any of them. She had bought her gymnasium suit with a bill from that pitifully small roll handed to her by her father. She had no money to buy another. She could not bring herself to confess this to Nan or Sadie and she would not confess it to her father, who would probably sacrifice something he needed himself to send her the money.

"No, you will just have to grin and bear it, Jo, old girl," she told herself, and added ruefully: "The hardest part of that is the grin!"

Things were still at this pass when Jessie Robinson burst in upon the chums one night, her dark eyes flashing.

"Girls, I've just heard the most abominable thing!" she cried. "I'm so mad I could bite!"

CHAPTER XVII

A SECRET CLUB

"As long as you don't bite us, Jessie!" said Nan pacifically. "Here!" pushing a box of candy toward the irate one, "have a bon-bon and see if you can't calm down."

"I don't want to calm down!" cried Jessie Robinson, sinking into a chair and wrathfully pounding the arms of it with her fists. "I won't ever calm down again and neither will you when you hear what I have to say!"

"I bet it's about Kate or Lottie," guessed Jo.

Jessie stared at her.

"How did you know?"

Jo chuckled mirthlessly.

"Everything horrid comes from them," she explained.

"Well, this is horrid! It's the worst I ever heard— —"

"Stop stammering and shoot," commanded Nan slangily, helping herself calmly to a bon-bon. "You might as well break the awful news and have it over with."

Jessie leaned forward and fixed the girls with her flashing eyes.

"It is about Kate and that awful Lottie," she said. "They are going around telling everybody that you girls are at the bottom of this second 'practical joke'!"

The three chums were on their feet at once, staring incredulously at Jessie.

"But how do you know they are saying that?" demanded Sadie.

"Doris heard of it first," answered Jessie. "And just now two of the younger girls came to me with the story. Where are you going?" she demanded suddenly as Jo started for the door.

"To Miss Romaine!" returned Jo, her lips set. "I'm going to ask her to make them stop it!"

As she turned to the door again, about to put her purpose into action, there came a timid knock.

"Some one's calling," said Nan.

"Maybe Lottie or Kate," Sadie suggested, her eyes flashing.

Jo pulled the door open quickly and disclosed a timid, shrinking figure in the hall. Almost before she had identified this figure as Lily Darrow the girl slipped within the room and pulled the door shut behind her.

Amazed, the girls stared at their unexpected visitor.

Lily was trembling. Her face was white. Yet she spoke with a feverish haste that was at odd variance with her frail appearance.

"I have only a minute to stay. I suppose I should not have come at all," she began, while the girls mutely regarded her. "I have just heard what Kate and Lottie are saying about you girls." She took a step forward and held out her hand to them appealingly.

"You can believe me or not— —"

"Of course we believe you, Lily," said Nan in pity for the girl's intense agitation.

Lily sent her a glance of gratitude and hurried on feverishly.

"I want you to know that I have no part in that awful story they are spreading," she said. "I don't believe it, and I—I'd stop it if I could. That's all—I just wanted you to know—and please—please—" She spread out her hands again appealingly. "Please don't let them know that I have been here!"

She turned then and before any one of the others could recover sufficiently from their astonishment to stop her, had run swiftly from the room.

"How she hates those two girls!" cried Sadie.

"And yet she stays with them and lets them bully her," added Nan. "It's beyond me!"

"I wish we could help her," said Jo thoughtfully. "I've a notion she needs help very badly."

"Why in the world do Kate Speed and Lottie pick on us?

Why should they say that we're playing silly practical jokes?" demanded Sadie. "It gets me!"

"Goosie!" snapped Jessie. "Don't you know they've never forgiven you for getting this room that they thought they'd already cabbaged?"

Jo would still have put her plan into action. By going to Miss Romaine she would probably stop the contemptible rumor set afoot by Kate and her friends. But this would not be a final victory, as Jessie succeeded in pointing out to the impulsive girl.

"They would say you were hiding behind the skirts of authority, or some such thing," she said. "No, I have a better plan."

When questioned she thus divulged it.

"We'll scare them. That's what we'll do!" she said. "A bunch of us girls will 'wait upon' Kate and Lottie as the old saying goes. We'll tell them that if they don't keep still we'll blind-fold them and make them walk the plank. If there are enough of us we ought to turn the trick."

Such methods were risky, as none knew better than the conspirators.

"Still, if we choose the right time and place we ought to get by with it all right," Nan decided, after some talk on the subject.

"And if we don't, then will be time enough to go to Miss Jane," added Jo.

The secret club called itself the "Knights of Darkness" and giggled a great deal in private over the title.

Rumors of this club—to which only a special few were admitted—came to the ears of Kate and Lottie, who were hurt because they had not been invited to join. So when two notes reached them mysteriously one day they joyfully prepared to obey the summons contained therein.

So ran the nonsensical contents:

"At fifteen minutes to twelve on Friday night next meet the gathering of ghosts in the haunted cellar beneath the house. Be prompt and make no noise lest ghosts shall take to heel and naught remain."

The signature was a drawing of an irregular figure attired as far as could be ascertained in something resembling a pillow slip.

The "haunted cellar" was, of course, the gymnasium, and in this promptly at quarter to twelve on Friday night a ghostly company assembled. The figures were arrayed in sheets that persisted in getting under their feet and tripping them, much to the giggling delight of the wearers.

"Sh-h!" cried one of them in a muffled whisper. "Here they come! Make a circle around them now and don't let either of them out!"

So Kate Speed and Lottie Sparks were surrounded by as ghostly a company as ever haunted a school gymnasium on a Friday night.

The speaker for the ghosts, who was none other than Jessie Robinson, well disguised, said in a deep voice:

"We are here assembled to bid you welcome and farewell!"

An unghostlike giggle came from the circle of white-enshrouded figures.

But Lottie and Kate did not giggle. They were palpably nervous. The gymnasium beyond the light provided by matter-of-fact electric torches in the muffled hands of the ghosts was filled with disturbing shadows. They thought of the thieves who had twice robbed the gymnasium and began to wish themselves safe back in bed.

The deep voice of the speaker continued.

"You are hereby warned, oh you livers upon earth—" Another giggle. "Livers" sounded funny "like something a chicken has," Sadie afterward explained—"that ghostly eyes are watching you. In other words," with a sudden fierce vindictiveness one does not usually associate with ghosts, "we have heard the horrid tales you have been spreading about the chums from Woodford, Kate Speed and Lottie Sparks. We like those girls, you two miserable sneaks— —"

"Hear! Hear!" from the circle of "ghosts" while the captives, realizing the trap they had fallen into, made a break for liberty.

"Hold 'em, ghosts!" said the deep voice of the speaker, and the ghostly ring pressed tighter about the now thoroughly frightened Kate and Lottie.

"We are not going to hurt you now!" Jessie's voice was once more menacing as she advanced upon the cowering girls. "But we're watching you, and the next time you say anything mean or sneaky, the least you'll get will be a ducking in the lake. Now, just remember that!"

There was a cry from two of the "ghosts" as the captives again made a dash for liberty.

"Let 'em go," said the speaker, in sepulchral tones. "And we, too, will vanish into those mysterious realms of ether from which we came. Farewell!"

When Lottie and Kate had finally disappeared, the ghosts disrobed amid a chorus of giggles.

"Well, that ought to fix 'em," Sadie said.

"But it won't make them love us any more," prophesied Jo.

"We'll have to look out for trouble from that quarter," Nan agreed, and added stoutly: "But you may be sure we'll be ready for it when it comes!"

By a miracle of good luck the conspirators managed to get up to their rooms undetected. They fell asleep chuckling at the thought of Kate Speed and Lottie Sparks and their chagrin.

The Knights of Darkness, once formed, was not disbanded. The girls enjoyed their secret club and their secret watchword, and more than anything else they enjoyed the curiosity their organization aroused in the girls who were not members of it.

They even took up a collection and sent away for club pins, an emblem of skull and cross bones over which they giggled delightedly in the privacy of their rooms.

The club so far was limited to the three girls from

Woodford, Jessie Robinson, Doris Maybel, Gladys Holt and four other chums of Jessie's, who remained its leader.

The midnight scare had the desired effect upon Lottie and Kate. They no longer circulated scandalous rumors about the three chums from Woodford. But those same girls suspected that this signified, not peace, but an armed neutrality, and that they would, in all probability, hear from these two unpleasant girls again.

Meanwhile, beyond saying that they might set a guard at the school, the local police, represented by Sheriff Crabb, accomplished nothing whatever toward the apprehension of the rascals who had twice plundered Laurel Hall.

As days went by and still there was no news of the thieves or their stolen property, the girls accepted the inevitable and settled down to studies and play much the same as usual.

As soon as the weather definitely cleared Sadie declared her intention of taking out a rowboat on the lake.

"But you don't know a thing about rowing!" protested Jo.

"What has that got to do with it? I can learn, can't I?"

"Well, for that matter, so can I," retorted Jo, and the two girls ran blithely up to the Hall to gain the consent of Miss Talley to take one of the boats on the lake.

Since the young teacher happened to be disengaged at the moment, she offered to go out with them.

"Oh, would you?" cried Sadie. "That will be fine! I do so want to know how to row."

Miss Talley, warmed by her enthusiasm, smiled.

"You shall," she promised.

So while Nan improved her service on the tennis courts in company with another first-year girl who thought Nan's game "simply marvelous," Jo and Sadie took their first rowing lesson.

The lake was beautiful in the glare of the afternoon sun. As the girls pushed off from the dock, Sadie holding one pair of oars, the young teacher the other, it seemed to them that they were embarking upon a lake of gold.

Sadie blissfully followed the instructions of Miss Talley, her face radiant with happiness.

"I could do this all my life!" she said.

Miss Talley smiled.

"You may feel differently when your hands are blistered," she said prosaically. "You may take my oars in a few moments," she added to Jo, "and I'll show you how to row together."

After an hour or so of practice that was undiluted joy to the two girls the teacher was pleased to praise her pupils and to predict that they would make rapid progress.

"We always have a rowing match sometime around the middle of October—before winter drives us indoors," she said, as they touched the dock again. "If you girls work hard, perhaps you may qualify to enter the race. Would you like that?"

"Would we!" they cried together, and again Miss Talley smiled at their enthusiasm.

CHAPTER XVIII

THE TENNIS MATCH

On their way to the Hall to wash and rest after their rather strenuous exercise on the lake, Jo and Sadie encountered Nan, racket in hand, just leaving the courts.

Nan's face was flushed and she was smiling with some secret enjoyment.

"Girls, I'm glad you came back," she greeted them eagerly. "I've the funniest thing to tell you."

She waited to divulge "the funniest thing," however, until they had reached the privacy of their own room. Then Nan threw her racket on the bed and pirouetted gleefully about the room.

"What do you suppose Kate Speed has done now?" she cried, stopping before her astonished chums.

"Anything for the K. of D. to get excited about?" asked Jo, eyebrows raised.

"Not yet," chuckled Nan. "She's challenged me to a tennis match, to find out who's the better man—I should say, girl."

"I could tell her that without any old tennis match," said Sadie loyally, and in her exuberance Nan hugged her.

"Well, but it will be a lark!" she cried. "I'll enjoy nothing better than licking Kate Speed properly in the open—with the whole school—more or less—looking on."

"Sure," said Jo. "But suppose you get walloped yourself, Nan? What then?"

Nan snapped her lingers airily.

"I refuse to consider impossibilities," she retorted haughtily, then giggled and hugged them both again. "Oh, girls, it will be fun! This is my chance to put that conceited Kate Speed out of the running for good and all!"

Although they were passionately loyal to Nan, the other girls were not so sure that their chum was a match for Kate Speed on the courts.

There was one thing Kate Speed could do exceptionally well—and that was play tennis. She was, they considered, a more brilliant player than Nan, although Nan was steadier and could keep her head much better in emergencies.

While it would be a great triumph if Nan should win—how would they feel if she lost?

"There would be no living in the same school with Kate Speed then," said Jo, as she discussed this unpleasant possibility with Sadie. "All in all, Sade, I'm not overanxious for the match day to come."

"Nor I!" agreed Sadie ruefully.

But as the day of the match had been set for Saturday, then only three days distant, the girls had scant time, fortunately, to nurse their gloomy forebodings.

The school was all agog over the coming clash between the two who had been rivals on the tennis courts almost since the opening day of the year at Laurel Hall.

Popular sentiment was in Nan's favor. The majority of the students wanted her to win. But there were some—faithful satellites of the rich girl—who were rooting against her.

As Saturday approached one thing became certain—that, no matter which side they favored, practically all the students of Laurel Hall would turn out to see the match.

Saturday morning Jo and Sadie woke up with a terrible weight of anxiety on their hearts.

Not so Nan. Usually the most modest of girls, in this instance she seemed absolutely sure of herself. There appeared not a doubt in her mind but what she could "wallop" Kate with the greatest ease.

Saturday morning fled by. Luncheon came, was over. Two o'clock—the time set for the match—approached.

Jo and Sadie tried gamely to hide their trepidation from Nan, but they were so nervous during the last hour that they ran away and hid until it should be time to accompany Nan to the courts.

They came back five minutes before the time to find Nan testing her racket and confidently smiling.

"Where have you girls been keeping yourselves?" she asked as they came in. "I've been waiting for a quarter of an hour. All set? Let's go."

They went, and at the edge of the campus were met by a group of Nan's friends and loyal adherents. By these they were borne triumphantly to the courts.

Kate was there before them, engaged in animated conversation with a group of her followers.

She frowned as she saw Nan, though Nan nodded and smiled with the friendliness of one sportsman to another. For the moment Kate was not Kate to Nan—an enemy whom it would be a joy to defeat. She was for the time only a worthy antagonist against whose undoubted ability she was testing her own.

The school had turned out for the occasion. The court was surrounded by girls eager to see the fray. Some of them were standing, but for the most part they were seated crosslegged on the ground, hugging their knees and gleefully discussing the possibilities of the coming match.

The two girls most concerned approached the contest in characteristically opposite manner.

Nan came on the court smiling, the racket in her left hand, her right extended to clasp Kate's across the net.

Kate, on the contrary, made no motion to meet Nan half-way. She scowled and ignored the outstretched hand of her antagonist.

Nan flushed and quickly lowered her hand.

There was an angry buzz about the courts, and one or two of Nan's supporters cried out:

"For shame! Do you call that sportsmanship?"

But Nan was smiling again gayly.

On her toes she danced back to her end of the court, taking her position about eight feet back of the net and to the right. For

Nan was essentially a net player; although she had been known, in doubles with a partner who was also a net player, to cover the line with great success.

Now, however, she chose the more familiar position, for she was determined to beat Kate Speed.

"All right, Kate!'" she cried, swinging her racket. "First serve yours!"

"She's foolish," cried Jo. "Here she starts with the sun full in her eyes and gives Speedy Kate first serve."

She half rose to her feet as though to remonstrate with Nan, but Sadie pulled her back again.

"Let her alone," she cried. "Nan knows what she's doing."

"Let's hope so!" muttered Jo, and, frowning, sat back on her heels to watch the play.

Kate Speed accepted the generosity of her adversary without protest—as the Kate Speeds of this world will always accept as their right any advantage offered them.

Nan waited, alert, half-turned from the net, both feet planted firmly on the ground, her racket ready.

Kate tossed the ball and with the weight of her body behind the stroke, sent a smashing service into the far left-hand corner of the court.

Running swiftly, Nan was there before the ball, and, with a lightning stroke slashed it over the net and almost at Kate's feet. Kate, dancing nimbly backward, struck at the ball, but not quite quickly enough. It fell into the net, and a triumphant cry came from Nan's supporters.

"Love fifteen!"

Kate's face burned a dull red. She would not look at Nan as she retrieved the ball.

From that on action was swift and furious.

Nan served and Kate smashed the ball back over the net to be met by a clever backhand stroke from Nan that sent Kate scurrying toward her base line. On her toes Kate reached for the ball and got it. Her smashing return caught Nan off guard. Her racket twanged with the impact of the ball, but the shot was low.

"Fifteen all," said Kate, and treated her adversary to a glance of triumph.

The sun was worrying Nan. She wished that she had brought her eyeshade.

Jo saw the swift motion of hand across sun-dazzled eyes and was on her feet in an instant.

"I'm going up to the room for something," she explained to Sadie.

But when she returned, Nan's sun shade dangling, Jo found she was too late. Kate, playing like one inspired, had won three points in rapid succession and with them had captured the first game.

Joe ran to Nan with the eyeshade, which her chum accepted gratefully.

"Thanks, Jo," she said, with a rueful smile. "I should have had this during the last game!"

But even the eyeshade failed to turn the tide. Kate was in better form than they had ever seen her. She seemed all over the court at once. She developed an uncanny accuracy in placing her shots where her adversary was not!

Nan appeared confused, dazzled by Kate's brilliant play. The score now stood 4-0 in favor of Kate.

Kate's cronies were jubilant; Nan's friends correspondingly downhearted.

"Kate's sort of cast a spell over her," Sadie worried. "I wish we could do something to wake her up."

"Never mind," said Jessie Robinson, who had come up and seated herself beside the chums. "Just watch out for a big comeback!"

This prophecy was soon, to some extent, justified. Nan drew herself together and, with lips set doggedly, wrenched the next two games from Kate.

They were won by "the skin of her teeth," as she afterward admitted. But they were won, and they certainly made the score look a little better. It stood now 4-2, in favor of Kate.

"Go it, Nan! Go it!" cried her friends from the sidelines, and Nan waved her racket at them cheerfully.

But their pleasure was short-lived. Kate won the next two games swiftly and with apparent ease.

"Game and set!" she cried, and triumphantly flung her racket over the net.

In changing courts it was necessary for Nan to pass close to the spot where Jo and Sadie and Jessie were seated.

"Nan," Jo cried in a pleading voice, "don't let Kate win! You can beat her!"

"Jo," said Nan, turning a set face to her chum, "let me tell you a secret. I'm going to!"

As Nan passed on Jo sank back on her heels again and gripped Sadie's hand hard.

"She's riled, Sade! Watch out now! I bet we see some fireworks!"

And they did!

Nan possessed one great asset, and that was that she played best when losing. Something stubborn and indomitable rose up in her and refused to submit to defeat.

As she faced Kate for the first game of the second set, Jo and Sadie saw this change in her. Their eyes shone.

"She's caught her stride!" Jo whispered. "Now, Speedy Kate, look out!"

CHAPTER XIX

NAN TRIUMPHS

It was a hard-fought set.

Nan won the first two games, catching Kate off her guard by the fury of her offensive.

In the third Kate rallied and won a game. But when Nan won the next three in succession her adversary began to crumple.

"The sun's in my eyes," she complained.

"I had it during the first set," Nan reminded her; and added, as she returned to her position behind the net: "Pull your eyeshade lower."

Kate glowered and fussed with her shade. But there were already impatient, half-jeering cries of "play ball" from the sidelines, and Kate could delay no longer.

She was playing in a petulant mood, and she fairly gave that last game to Nan.

"Game and set!" cried Nan, and a frenzy of cheering broke from the crowd of girls.

Nan ventured a word of caution to Kate as they passed each other in changing courts.

"Don't let yourself get mad," she said, in a low tone. "It's spoiling your game."

"You let my game alone!" snapped Kate. "The sun was in my eyes, that's what was the matter! I'll beat you this time or know the reason why!"

Nan shrugged her shoulders and flexed her racket.

"Try and do it!" was her challenge, for Nan was once more sure of herself.

The first game justified her confidence.

Unlike Nan, who was at her best when losing, Kate, when

losing, was at her worst. As one of the girls had remarked about her once:

"It's mighty hard to get Kate running down hill in a tennis game, but when you do, she seems in an all-fired hurry to reach the bottom!"

And so it seemed now. Nan won three games without half trying.

Kate came back in a flash of fury in the third, brought the game to forty love, and then succumbed to Nan's superior coolness.

Toward the end of the fifth game—and Nan's fifth victory—Sadie, Jo and Jessie Robinson exchanged glances.

"This isn't a match," grinned Jessie, putting the general thought into words. "This is slaughter!"

Toward the end of the sixth game when the score stood love forty and Nan was still working in fine form, Kate went to pieces. In a rage, she flung the racket from her, ran to the grassy bank that bordered the court, sank down upon it and burst into loud sobs.

"I'm sick! That's what's the matter with me!" she cried to the girls who crowded around her in consternation. "How can I play when I'm so sick I can hardly stand on my feet."

Here was a nice how-to-do!

Nan pushed her way through the crowd and looked down upon her fallen enemy.

"I'm sorry you're sick," she said gravely. "I'll wait if you like until you can get a drink of water and pull yourself together."

"A drink of water! That's what the whole trouble is!"

The strident voice belonged to Lottie Sparks, and the spectators crowded closer, sensing battle.

"There's been some shady work going on here," cried Lottie, and even Kate lifted a furious, tear-stained face to stare at her chum.

Nan took a quick step forward.

"What do you mean by that?" she asked quietly of Lottie Sparks.

"I mean that some one put something in a glass of water Kate took before she came out," said Lottie, carrying her bluff through with a bravado that hid a tremor of fright. "And the girl who did it is the one I'm looking at just now!"

Every one turned to follow the direction of Lottie's suddenly fixed gaze. She was staring straight at Sadie Appleby!

There was a moment of complete silence, the silence of stupefaction. Then several of the girls turned vengefully upon Lottie Sparks.

"The sneak! Make her eat her words!"

"A ducking in the lake is what she ought to have!"

Lottie, casting one terrified glance at the unfriendly, scowling faces of her schoolmates, realized that she had gone too far and, turning, broke through the ring of outstretched hands.

She raced toward the lake with practically the whole school after her!

Lottie reached the dock at the shore of the lake, ran down it breathless, with a number of girls in hot pursuit.

A rowboat lay moored at the end of the dock, and toward this she raced. Her pursuers guessed her intention.

"Don't let her get away!" they cried. "Catch her before she cuts the boat loose!"

Probably the cries of her pursuers, so close upon her, rattled Lottie. At any rate, in reaching to untie the knot in the rope that held the boat to the dock, she lost her balance and plunged heels over head into the lake.

The other girls stood aghast at this mishap.

It was probably lucky for them, if not for Lottie, that things turned out this way. For as Lottie, sputtering and blowing, came to the surface, the girls noticed that several teachers were hurrying from the direction of the Hall.

Certainly, it was no laughing matter now!

Lottie dragged herself into the rowboat that she had missed by a few inches. She was a sorry spectacle indeed, with her hair matted close to her head and her clothes dripping lake water.

As the teachers—there were three of them, Miss Blitz, Miss

Tully and Madame Briais—reached the dock, the girls stepped back respectfully and Lottie set up a loud wail.

"They pushed me over! They tried to drown me! They'd like to see me drowned, the horrid old things!"

This would have sounded funny to the girls if the accusation had not verged on the truth. They had no thought of drowning Lottie, of course. That accusation was absurd. Nor had they pushed her into the lake. But they had been pursuing her in no friendly spirit.

Miss Tully, who rather dominated the other teachers of the school when Miss Romaine was not present, commanded the girls sharply:

"You will all go to the Hall and to your rooms until we learn the truth of this disgraceful proceeding. Lottie Sparks," turning to the girl who was trying to wring some of the moisture from her sodden garments, "go up to the house and change your clothes. Then report at Miss Romaine's office. She will hear your story."

Madame Briais started forward as though she intended to speak, but Miss Tully silenced her with a grim look.

Smarting under a sense of injustice, the girls trooped back to the Hall, talking gloomily about the episode and wondering what the outcome would be. The one bright spot was Lottie's ducking.

"She deserved a good horsewhipping for saying such a thing!" Jo cried heatedly. "The idea of accusing you, Sadie! Now if she had said it of me——"

"She has hated me especially ever since I hit her with that muddy tennis ball," said Sadie. "I suppose this was her chance to get even."

Other girls grouped themselves about Nan and Sadie, sympathizing with them both.

"Anyway, you won the match," Gladys Holt said to Nan. "The last game went to you by default and gave you the set 6-0."

"I don't like taking games by default," Nan said, frowning. "If she had played for a few minutes longer I could have honestly claimed the match. As it is—" she shrugged her shoulders and did not finish the sentence.

When they reached their room the three chums were in a gloomy frame of mind.

"I suppose we'll receive a summons from the office soon," said Jo, walking excitedly up and down the floor. "And, moreover, we'll have to answer to all sorts of trumped up charges. I wish Lottie Sparks and Kate Speed could be run out of Laurel Hall!"

The chums had not long to wait for the expected summons from the office.

Nan and Sadie alone were wanted. Jo, it seemed, was not implicated this time.

"I wonder what made her leave me out," said the latter dryly. "Lottie and Kate usually try to get the three of us in a jam together. This must be an oversight!"

"Wish us good luck, anyway," Sadie said, as she and Nan prepared to answer the summons. "We may not come up alive!"

But in Miss Romaine's office the two girls found a very different spectacle from the one they had expected.

Miss Romaine was sitting behind her desk and there was an unusual gravity on her handsome face.

Kate was there, looking subdued and sullen. Jessie Robinson and Doris Maybel were standing beside the desk. But what surprised Nan and Sadie most was the sight of Lottie Sparks cowering in one of the mahogany chairs, dissolved in tears.

Miss Romaine greeted the newcomers and motioned them to her.

"I have investigated the charge brought against you by Lottie Sparks," she said quietly. "I thought it best to do so before sending for you girls at all. There are many witnesses—in fact, almost all the girls in the school," she added, with a slight smile, "who are not only willing but eager to testify in your behalf. These were eye witnesses, and they declare that you had nothing to do with Lottie's mishap. That she slipped and fell in the lake herself."

"But they were chasing me! They made me fall in," cried Lottie, through her tears.

"And why?" cried Miss Romaine, so sternly that even Sadie and Nan stepped back from her and Lottie actually trembled, cowering back in her chair. "Because you made a contemptible—a wicked—accusation which you have also confessed to me was false! I will not repeat it here for the sake of Sadie Appleby whom I know to be an honest, upright girl.

"And now," the teacher added briskly, "I want you to apologize to Sadie, and to Nan Harrison also for implicating her in your charge. Come, Lottie," as the latter made no move to obey. "I am waiting!"

There was a ring in the last words that compelled obedience.

Lottie Sparks wiped her eyes and looked up sullenly.

"I—I'm—sorry," she said, as though the words choked her. "I was—mad about Kate's losing the match. I hardly knew what I was saying."

"That's all right," Sadie could be generous to a fallen enemy. "As long as you're sorry, I don't care. I guess none of the girls believed what you said, anyway."

"They certainly didn't act as though they did," Jessie said, with a grin.

Miss Romaine raised her hand.

"I would be sorry to believe any of my girls lacking in good sportsmanship," she said gravely. "Games should not be played so much for the sake of winning as for the sake of the game itself. I hear that you two girls," she looked from Nan to the sullen, fuming Kate, "played some excellent tennis this afternoon. You lost, Kate, but you must learn to take defeat with a smile. I want you to shake hands with Nan and congratulate her on her success."

CHAPTER XX

CAUGHT IN THE SWAMP

The closer friends of the three chums from Woodford declared afterward that they had been sure Kate would balk at shaking hands with Nan.

"I never thought she would do it," Nan herself said, in relating the incident to Jo afterward. "When I saw her come forward and take my hand, I honestly thought I'd faint! The surprise was almost too much for your Nan!"

However, Miss Romaine had a way of compelling obedience, even from girls like Kate.

The congratulations were performed with a poor grace, to be sure, but they were performed. The moment was one of victory for Nan and of defeat for Kate.

Yet the latter stepped back with a toss of her head that declared her far from subdued yet. She flashed a look at Nan that was full of enmity.

"I'll get even," said the look. "You just wait!"

After a few more words about the admirable quality of good sportsmanship, Miss Romaine dismissed them.

Nan and Sadie, with Jessie and Doris, made at once for their room where they poured the whole story into Jo's sympathetic and anxious ear.

"Glory be!" cried the latter, turning a hand-spring of delight and landing in some mysterious manner upon the bed. "The ship is ours again! The enemy is routed! All's well with the world!"

"Don't crow too soon," warned Sadie dubiously. "Those two can bear watching, let me tell you."

But for some time after the incident of the match it looked as though Kate and Lottie were effectually subdued.

Following the match came a quiet Sunday and then two

weeks of hard work in the classrooms. The three chums were doing well, although Sadie had hard work to keep up in mathematics and Nan rather lagged in her French. Jo went along swimmingly except for a little "flop," as she expressed it, in physics.

During those days letters came from home. Nan's Aunt Emma was doing as well as could be expected, but Nan could understand from her mother's letter that the family had hoped the invalid would improve following her act of standing on her feet during the fire scare.

"Oh, if only she could stand again—and walk!" exclaimed Nan to her chums.

"Wouldn't it be grand!" returned Sadie.

"It's queer the doctors can't do something," breathed Jo.

Poor Jo had her own sorrow—and the others knew it and sympathized with her thoroughly. Mr. Morley was struggling to make both ends meet. And so far nothing had been seen or heard of Andrew Simmer, the rascally fellow who had caused the trouble.

"I feel almost as if I ought to go home and help Mother," said Jo, more than once.

"No, you had better stay here and get a good education," replied Nan. "In the end, that may help more than anything else. With a good education you'll stand a better chance of earning good money."

The second Saturday after the tennis match was a beautiful day—one of those warm fall days that seems an echo of mid-summer. Since the chums from Woodford and some of their friends had been planning all week for a row up the lake with a picnic at the farther end of it, they greeted the dawn of this perfect Saturday joyfully and as one that had been made especially for their outing.

Sadie and Jo had kept up their practice with the oars and were by this time as enthusiastic over it as Nan was over tennis. They were becoming very skillful, and were impatiently awaiting Miss Talley's announcement as to the exact day of the proposed boat races.

"In the meantime, we'll show you how good we are," said Jo, as the chums joyfully shouldered lunch baskets and started down to the dock.

There were several boatloads of girls who set off on the picnic that fine Saturday, eager to enjoy the last outing of the sort they would, perhaps, have before cold weather settled down upon them.

"This time of year the weather may change over night," said Gladys Holt, as she put a fuzzy white sweater into the boat she and her chums had appropriated. "To-morrow we may be wondering how we ever had the nerve to come out to-day!"

The boats were, many of them—most of them, in fact—built with a double set of oars and oar-locks. Two boats of this sort the Woodford girls and their friends chose for the trip up the lake.

"Jo and I'll do the work," said Sadie to Nan. "You sit in the stern and look handsome, Nan."

"If I sit in the stern I ought to look stern," retorted Nan, and at this feeble witticism the girls laughed happily. It was the kind of day that made them laugh at almost anything!

"Don't let's follow the crowd," called Jessie, as her boat, safely launched, floated out upon the bright surface of the lake. "Let's be original."

"Right-o," agreed Jo. "Where'll we go?"

"To Huckleberry Island." It was Gladys Holt who spoke this time from the neighboring boat, and she accompanied the words by a gesture of the hand that indicated the black outline of an island far up the lake. "Follow us, and you'll never repent it."

With a laughing wave of her hand, Jo assented. But Sadie looked troubled.

"Huckleberry Island is a long distance up the lake," she said. "I don't think Miss Romaine would want us to go so far."

"Oh, we've the whole day before us," Nan urged, stretching luxuriously in the brilliant sunshine, like a kitten before a hearth. "Miss Jane won't care as long as we don't stay out too late."

"Away dull care and let's be gay!" sang Jo, breaking into the strains of a merry school song. The girls all joined her, and Sadie's protest was heard no more.

They rowed lazily, for, as Nan had said, they had the whole day before them. As they looked toward Laurel Hall they saw three more boatloads of merrymakers push off from the shore.

"They are making for Maple Island," called Doris from Jessie's boat.

"And Kate Speed's one of them," said Sadie, which, Nan suggested, more than half reconciled her to the long trip to Huckleberry Island.

They were more than half an hour on the trip up the lake and on the way they passed several other interesting and picturesque islands.

Nan sighed contentedly.

"I don't think there's another such beautiful spot on the face of the earth," she said.

"Well," judicially from Jo, "I haven't seen a great deal of the earth, but I'll tell it, right from where I sit, that this is good enough for me!"

They at last rounded a turn in the lake, and a shout from Jessie in the boat ahead warned them that they had reached Huckleberry Island.

This was really one of the largest islands in the lake and was well known, especially to those living in that vicinity, for at one end of the island was a large huckleberry swamp where the huckleberry bushes grew to unusual size. Earlier in the season these great bushes had been loaded with fruit, much to the delight of the many country folks who rowed over to the island to pick them.

"Here so soon!" cried Nan regretfully. "I could float like this all day."

Sadie looked at her severely.

"Going home, my dear, you will do some of the work!"

The boats came to rest in a tiny inlet where the gently shelving shore formed a perfect landing place.

"We'll tie the boats here and then go up to eat," Jessie Robinson stated. "I'm famished already."

As this seemed to be a state peculiar to them all, no one demurred, and they went at once in search of a pretty spot where they could spread their lunch.

They found the ideal place almost immediately—a level space abounding in flat rocks and commanding a good view of the lake.

"It's a lot better here than on the other end of the island," said Gladys, as she delved hungrily into one of the baskets. "Chicken sandwiches—hum! And chocolate cake—not so bad!"

"What's the matter with the other end of the island?" demanded Jo, through a mouthful of hard-boiled egg.

"There are huckleberry bushes—loads of 'em," Doris said.

"But they grow right in an awful swamp," Jessie added. "And if you don't watch your step, you're apt to get more swamp than huckleberries. Several people have tried it, and they know!"

"Sounds interesting," said Jo, rummaging for more hard-boiled eggs. "If we haven't enough lunch we can finish up on huckleberries—if there are any left."

When the contents of the baskets were exhausted she rose to make good her boast, despite the lazy protests of the girls.

"Sit down, can't you?" cried Gladys Holt. "The sight of so much energy makes me tired."

"The sight of so much sloth makes me tired!" retorted Jo severely. "If you want to sit there, like so many lizards basking in the sun, you may. Me, I'm going to hunt huckleberries!"

"We aren't lizards and there isn't any sun," retorted Doris. "And all the huckleberries you'll find at this time of year you can put in a thimble."

But Jo gave no sign that she heard. She was already disappearing through the trees.

Nan rose with a weary sigh and Sadie followed suit.

"I suppose we've got to go after her," said the latter plaintively. "There's no telling what she'd get into if left to her own devices!"

But Jo, hearing them, ran on ahead mischievously.

"I'll give them the hunt of their lives!" she chuckled. "The nerve of them! Talking as though I needed a nurse!"

A few moments later Sadie and Nan caught sight of her through the trees and gave full chase.

Laughing, breathless, looking over her shoulder at her pursuers, Jo did not notice her danger until it was too late! Almost before she knew it she was in the midst of the dangerous huckleberry swamp!

Her feet slipped from the firm earth into a slimy ooze. Mud and water clutched at her ankles, drawing her down deeper into the slime the more she struggled.

Jo looked about her wildly. On all sides rose huckleberry bushes, their branches now bare save for a few dried berries here and there.

"The huckleberry swamp!" she cried.

Nan and Sadie were running toward her. She called out a warning to them, but they did not understand—they thought she was still joking.

They did not understand until their feet, too, caught in the sticky ooze. Then the laughter on their faces froze into fear.

"I tried to warn you!" cried Jo, half-sobbing. "It's the swamp! I tried to warn you, but you ran straight on! Oh, why didn't you listen to me!"

Sadie tried to struggle and then gave a startled, strangled cry.

She had reached a deeper part of the marsh. She sank to her waist in muck and water and on her face was a look of stark panic that was terrible to see!

CHAPTER XXI

A REMEMBERED FACE

The next half hour proved to the three chums to be little less than a nightmare.

They had heard before of the treacherousness of a huckleberry swamp—there was such a swamp near their homes in which a boy and a girl had lost their lives—but never before had they realized what an inanimate monster such a swamp could be.

This present swamp was perhaps a quarter of a mile in diameter. It lay low near one end of the island and was surrounded by huckleberry bushes from four to seven and even eight feet in height—sturdy bushes that in mid-summer bent low with their loads of fruit. In the swamp were numerous other bushes, with here and there tufts of coarse swamp grass. Between these bushes and tufts of grass was the treacherous ooze and slime into which the girls were rapidly sinking.

The more they struggled to free themselves, the more deeply they were caught. Their cries for help brought no response.

In their merry chase over the island they had run farther from the picnic grounds than they had thought. Or perhaps the other girls, not as lazy as they had pretended, had wandered off in another direction, putting still greater distance between them and the unfortunate victims in the swamp.

Exhausted between their cries for help and their efforts to free themselves from the muck and slime, the three girl chums finally gave up and stared at each other in helpless despair.

"I guess we'll have to stay here like flies stuck on flypaper for the rest of our natural lives," said Nan resentfully.

"But suppose we should sink in still deeper?" wailed Sadie. "There isn't any solid bottom to this thing. We'll be k-killed!"

"Wait a minute!" in Jo's voice there was sudden hope. "There's a board over here. If I can only reach it— —"

What she had not seen before, half hidden as it was among the heavy bushes, was a board about a foot wide and seven or eight feet long. From the appearance of it, it seemed to have once been a part of a boat—an old boat probably drifted upon the island and long since fallen to pieces.

"If you can only get it without falling in up to your neck," Nan said anxiously. "Do be careful, Jo."

"My dear, as Miss Tully says, 'to be careful under such circumstances is a practical impossibility.' Still— —"

Reaching for the board, Jo slipped and almost fell. Nan and Sadie screamed and made an instinctive gesture toward her, only to flounder helplessly. The nightmare of it!

But Jo recovered herself and reached pluckily for the board again. This time she touched it and, with the tips of her fingers, drew it toward her.

"Jo, do you think it will bear your weight and not let you down into the mud again?"

"If it does we won't be any worse off than we are now," said Jo grimly. "Anyway, we've got to try something."

She tested their frail hope tentatively, then gave a cry of joy.

"Girls, the other end of it is on solid ground. I think we can make it!"

Here was good news. Jo had at least found where solid ground was.

Steadying herself by the board, Jo gradually managed to get one foot free. Gingerly she rested it upon the board. The board sank deep into the mud, even beneath that light weight.

"Suppose it should break!" cried Sadie, and Nan turned upon her in exasperation.

"Stop supposing!" she cried. "We can't afford it!"

Working as carefully and quickly as she could, Jo managed to get a foothold on the board before it became too deeply mired.

She ran lightly up it toward the part that rested on solid ground. The other girls watched her breathlessly.

If the board should break!

But it held! A moment more and Jo felt the blessed surety of solid earth beneath her feet.

"Hooray!" cried Nan. "Now you'd better run back and get that piece of rope in the boat. Something tells me we're going to need it."

"No, wait a minute. I think I can reach you with the board."

Dragging the board after her, Jo made her way cautiously around the swamp, feeling each foot of ground before she ventured to rest her weight upon it.

"There now!" she cried when she had come as near to her chums as she dared. "I'll shove it toward you, Nan, and you see if you can catch hold!"

Nan could not—quite. But after a desperate effort she managed to force herself forward the required inch or two until she felt her fingers upon the plank.

"Now, Sadie, see if you can't catch hold of Nan. Then I can pull you both out!"

Sadie struggled hard and finally managed to catch Nan's outstretched hand.

"Now!" cried Jo, clutching her end of the board firmly. "Heave ho, and I'll pull you ashore!"

There was a good deal of scrambling and puffing and panting before Nan, holding fast to the board, felt her foot strike upon solid ground.

The rest was easy, and it was only a moment before Sadie also had joined the two disheveled, mud-drenched girls on the edge of the swamp.

They eyed each other oddly for a moment, then broke into hysterical giggles.

"What are we going to do?" cried Nan. "We never can go back to the Hall looking like this."

"I guess we'll have to," said Jo practically. "We can't stay here all night. That's a sure thing."

"What we need is a fire," Sadie said, as they started to skirt the swamp and find their way to the picnic grounds. "If we could dry our clothes we might be able to scrape some of this awful mud off them."

"Speaking of fires!" cried Jo dramatically. "Look at this!"

The girls hurried up to her and found that "this" was the ashes of a recent campfire.

"Well, what of it?" said Sadie wonderingly. "It isn't so odd for people to build a campfire in the woods, is it?"

"No, but this campfire was built just recently—and put out only a short time ago," returned Jo, thoughtfully stirring some of the still smoldering embers with her foot. "And now I wonder," she added, looking oddly at her companions, "why these campers, whoever they were, didn't come to our aid when we called for help. They must have heard us!"

"Miss Keeneye on the job again," Nan began banteringly, but Sadie interrupted with a sudden exclamation.

"Look there!" she cried excitedly. "That motor boat—just putting off from shore!"

The launch came out from behind a jutting portion of the island almost directly beneath the spot where the girls were standing.

With a quick exclamation, Jo ran swiftly down to the water's edge, the better to view the occupants of the boat.

One of the men turned as his companion urged the launch to greater speed and Jo saw him distinctly. She drew back with a startled exclamation.

"What is it, Jo?" cried Nan, at her elbow. "You look as though you had seen a ghost."

"I've seen worse," said Jo, in a queer voice. "One of those men in the launch was Andrew Simmer!"

It took some time for Sadie and Nan to draw a coherent story from Jo's excited lips. Never having heard very much of Andrew Simmer before and knowing none of the details concerning Mr. Morley's business troubles, they naturally could guess no reason for Jo's excitement until she gave them the more important facts.

"I've got to follow him!" Jo cried frantically. "Some way, I've got to follow him and see where he goes. Oh, look!" she pointed excitedly out upon the lake. A second motor boat had come into view. "Behold an answer to prayer!"

Before either of her companions could guess her intention, she was hailing the occupants of the second motor boat.

"Help! Help!" she cried, making a megaphone of her hands. "Help! Come quick!"

"Good gracious, Jo!" cried Nan. "They'll think you're dying!"

"I am!" retorted Jo. "I'm dying of fear that Andrew Simmer will get away! Oh, joy, they're heading in here!"

As the motor boat put in toward the shore, Jo waded out to meet it. Nan and Sadie followed.

"We're soaked anyway," said the former philosophically. "And at least the water is clean. It will even wash off some of the mud."

"Goodness, look at Jo!" gasped Sadie. "She's getting into the boat."

"Well, what did you think she was going to do—sink it?" queried Nan. "Come on, Sade, we've got to see her through this!"

The occupants of the second motor boat were three young men. Though scarcely more than boys in years, they seemed very old and experienced to the three girl chums of Laurel Hall.

One of these strangers reached out a hand to Jo as she unceremoniously scrambled over the side of the boat. Nan and Sadie followed, each helped in turn.

"That boat!" cried Jo, pointing to the first launch, which was already some distance up the lake. "Catch it! Please catch it! There's a criminal in that boat! I've got to deliver him to justice! Can your launch make it?"

"Young lady, my boat can do anything," said the boy who held the steering wheel. "If you want to overhaul that boat, why, we'll overhaul that boat."

"Oh, please, please do!" cried Jo, almost beside herself with excitement. "Everything depends upon it! Everything!"

CHAPTER XXII

THE BOAT RACE

If the boys were amazed at the way these strange mud-bespattered girls tumbled into their boat and took possession of it, they were well-bred enough not to betray surprise.

Besides, they were interested in the chase, and for the moment all lesser matters were relegated to the background. They must catch that boat.

But the first launch had a good start of them, and, just as they seemed to be gaining upon it, the smaller boat dodged about one of the islands and was completely lost to view.

"Oh, did you see that!" cried Nan, in dismay.

"Now what are we going to do?" added Jo distractedly.

"What it takes to find that boat, we've got," grinned the boy at the wheel. "Don't you worry."

But, as it turned out, the pilot was overconfident. The first boat with the two men in it, one of whom Jo was sure was Andrew Simmer, had disappeared. Though they searched for it for some time—Jo would not give up—they were finally forced to admit that the pursued had been too clever for them.

"I suppose we might as well admit defeat," said Jo reluctantly at last. "Though I'd have given a million dollars—supposing I had it—to have overhauled that boat."

On the way back to Huckleberry Island the young folks, so strangely met, introduced themselves to each other.

The three boys were camping not far from Laurel Hall.

"We had to take our vacation late," said Fred Fielding, the lad at the wheel, "and now we are going to make the most of it. We won't go home until Nature gives us the cold shoulder and drives us out."

"It seems to me it's getting colder now," said Sadie, shivering.

"That's because you're all wet," said Dodd Martyn, another of the three boys. "If you want to dodge a good cold it's my opinion you'd better be getting home quick."

On this point all agreed. The fright the chums had experienced in the huckleberry swamp and the excitement afterward brought intense reaction. They wanted nothing better than to get back to the Hall to exchange wet clothes for dry and revel in the luxury of being once more warm and safe.

Frank Gibbs, the third of the trio of nice boys, pointed out an excellent landing place on Huckleberry Island near the spot that the girls had chosen for their picnic grounds. Here the young folks parted, the boys urging that they meet again soon to talk over the exciting events of the day.

It was not until after they had gone off in their motor launch that Jo remembered that she had not explained to them her reason for pursuing the man who looked like Andrew Simmer.

"And they never even asked me about it!" she marveled. "That's what I call being perfect gentlemen!"

At that moment Jessie Robinson, Doris Maybel and Gladys Holt rushed down upon them, demanding to know what they had been doing and what they meant by "scaring us to death."

"Let's g-go home," said Jo, her teeth chattering. "We'll explain everything on the way."

They hastily packed what was left of the contents of the lunch baskets and left the island.

With the two boats as close together as it was possible to get them, allowing for the space that must be left for the swing of the oars, Sadie told of their dreadful experience in the swamp and Jo recounted to an interested audience her belief as to the identity of the man she saw in the launch and her reasons for wanting to lay hands upon him.

"But, Jo, are you sure it was Andrew Simmer?" asked Nan excitedly.

"Not as sure as I was at the time," Jo answered truthfully.

"Still, I got a pretty good look at his face, and if one of those men in the boat wasn't Dad's missing clerk, then Andrew Simmer must have a double. Still, what's the use of talking," she added dolefully. "I've lost him now and I don't expect ever to see him again."

They rowed back to the Hall as quickly as they could, for it was growing cooler, and Jo, Sadie, and Nan were shivering in their wet clothes.

"I hope no one is about to see us land," Sadie said as they neared the dock.

"The only thing we need to make this day perfect is a meeting with Lottie and Kate just now," added Nan.

But in this they were fortunate. There were few girls on the campus when they landed at the dock and it was a comparatively simple matter to reach their room without attracting attention.

Jo was disconsolate.

"To think I came so near that Andrew Simmer," she mourned, "and then let him get away from me after all!"

She flung off her wet clothing, slipped on a dressing gown and sat down at the table near the window.

"What are you going to do?" Nan asked curiously.

"Write to Dad," Jo flung over her shoulder. "I'm going to tell him what I saw—or thought I saw—to-day and he can do as he thinks best about it."

Although Andrew Simmer—or the man Jo took to be him—formed the major part of the girls' conversation during the next few days, nothing came of that strange experience on the lake.

Meanwhile, Jo received letters from home that were anything but cheering. Her father was struggling heroically to save his business from utter ruin, and in the struggle was losing his health. That was what Jo read between the lines of her mother's resolutely cheerful letters and her father's brief scrawls. Neither of her parents seemed to attach much importance to her account of the man she had taken to be Andrew Simmer and as day followed day Jo herself began to believe that she must have been mistaken.

The good news came from Miss Emma. The latter wrote in glowing terms of improvement in the state of her health and her hope that before many months had passed she might be cured.

Then one day Jo received a cordial note of appreciation from Mrs. Harrison in which she said that Jo's weekly "journal" was playing an important part in the invalid's improvement, both physical and mental.

> "She is living her own youth over again through you, my dear," wrote Nan's mother. "She actually seems to be growing younger. She reads your letters again and again and laughs like a girl over them. Each day she tries to stand, and yesterday, for the first time, succeeded. For a full moment she stood by herself without support and has been greatly excited over it ever since. We now hope for her ultimate recovery, and if such a happy thing should come to pass, you, my dear girl, will be largely responsible for it. You seem to have given our poor invalid a new interest in life, and we are very, very grateful to you."

"As though I shouldn't be the grateful one!" thought Jo, as she folded the letter and put it back in the envelope. "They all seem to forget that!"

Meanwhile great preparations were being made for the boat races.

The contestants were divided into three classes—freshmen, sophomores and juniors. The seniors did not compete in these boat races, though they watched their under classmen with a great deal of interest.

Jo and Sadie were, of course, in the freshmen division, and as the day of the great test approached they became more and more determined to carry off the honors in their class.

On the afternoon before the day of the race Nan brought news.

"I overheard Lottie and Kate talking about to-morrow," she said. "Who do you think are going to enter the race—representing that crowd?"

"Who?" they asked together.

"Carol Haynes and Ruth Davis. They are the new girls that Kate and Lottie have won over to their side."

"That's so Kate can crow if Ruth and Carol win the race," Jo said, frowning.

"Sure!" chuckled Nan. "Kate can't win from me on the tennis courts, so she's getting some of her friends to beat you girls on the water."

"Well, it's up to us," said Jo, jamming her hands savagely into the pockets of her sport skirt, "to disappoint them!"

The morning of the great day dawned fair and rather cold.

"Just the day for a race!" Jo exulted. "Never felt in better form in my life!"

About two o'clock in the afternoon the girls turned out in full force to witness the boat race of the freshmen. The course of the race was from the boathouse to an island about half a mile distant; then around the island and back again to the starting point, making a little over a mile in all.

The girls in their bright-colored frocks were grouped along the shore of the lake like a border of fall flowers. They were talking and laughing in high spirits, calling gay greetings to each other.

Lily Darrow stood a little apart from the rest, so pale and quiet that more than once Kate spoke to her sharply and asked what she was "mooning" about.

Lily's reply to the last of these sharp queries was lost in a sudden cheering. The freshmen were lining up for the start.

"Go it, Jo! Go it, Sadie!" cried Nan.

Kate shot a venomous look at Nan and shrilled in a voice that carried above the rest:

"Beat 'em, Carol! Beat 'em, Ruth!"

"You can do it! Go to it!" added Lottie Sparks.

CHAPTER XXIII

A CLOSE BATTLE

Miss Talley, in a boat by herself, with the four competing boats lined up on either side of her, gave the signal for the start.

They had drawn lots for position, and to Jo and Sadie had fallen the poorest of all. They were on the outside—the boat nearest the shore. Consequently they would be on the outer rim of the fleet as it rounded the island.

This did not worry them so much as the fact that Carol and Ruth had drawn best position. Jo and Sadie felt fairly confident that they could beat the other entrants, but they were not so sure about Ruth and Carol. They had watched these girls work and knew they were good. Now, with the added advantage of a good position, it looked as though their rivals would win.

Then came the wild burst of cheering from shore. Nan's words came clearly to her chums. So did the cry of Lottie Sparks!

The two girls whose boat held the worst position in the line-up, stiffened.

"We'll beat them, Jo!" cried Sadie.

"Do or die!" returned Jo.

"Now, girls!" called Miss Talley. "Ready!"

In her hand was the string attached to the toy cannon that was to give them their signal to start. There was a loud boom and eight pairs of oars struck the water at the same instant.

The watchers on shore drew a quick breath. They leaned forward eagerly. Lottie's eye caught Jessie's. She made a gesture toward the lake and grinned meaningly. Jessie frowned and pointedly turned her back.

"They're off!" Nan gripped her arm. "Oh, look, Jessie, our girls are falling behind!"

"They'll make it up," Jessie countered stoutly. "There's good stuff in those girls. There they go! Watch 'em!"

For Sadie, acting as stroke—the girls of Laurel Hall liked to make their boat races as much like a college shell race as possible—had increased the steady motion of the oars. Left behind at the start, Sadie and Jo were catching up, slowly, it is true, but seemingly surely.

"They'll never make it, though!" Excited as she was, Nan kept her voice low so as not to reach the unfriendly ears of Kate's crowd. "They have the outside, you see, and going around the island they will lose more than they can possibly gain later."

"If they're wise they can cut in," Doris spoke quickly, pointing toward the island.

"That's right!" cried Gladys Holt. "There's one place where they can cross over——"

"If some one doesn't guess their intention and beat them to it," said Jessie, between set teeth. "My, but that's good work! Watch 'em go!"

Nan said nothing. Her heart was beating fast. She knew that spot where the girls "if they were smart" could cut across and come home on the inside of the course.

But she knew also the danger of such a strategic move. Close to the island the waters of the lake were shallow. There was the danger of being upset or of grounding the boat—either of which mishaps would mean the loss of the race and the ridicule of their enemies.

"Oh, if they can only do it! If they can only do it!" Nan said over and over to herself as she beat her hands one upon the other and stared after the racing boats. "I wish Jo were stroke. She'd manage the trick some way."

But in this she did Sadie an injustice. Sadie might not be as good as either of her chums on the tennis courts. But in a boat, with the oars in her hand, she was a different person.

They had reached the island. Ruth and Carol were in the lead, with two of the other boats trailing close behind. Sadie and Jo brought up the rear. A poor chance for victory, it would seem, with Jo and Sadie apparently quite out of the race.

But this was far from the fact. Sadie had deliberately

allowed her boat to fall behind so that she would be able to seize the desired opening when it came.

It came!

"All ready, Jo?" called Sadie softly.

"Ready!" returned Jo.

They had reached that portion of the lake where the water off shore was deepest. A gap showed between the third boat and the island. It was through this gap that Sadie and Jo must force their boat if they hoped to make the inside of the course.

Having conserved their strength, they had it for use now. Swiftly their oars flashed in the water. Rapidly the gap closed up between them and the leading boat. They worked as they had never worked before, bending their backs to the task.

Carol and Ruth guessed their intention—but too late.

They tried to close in that gap between them and the island, but before they succeeded, Sadie had nosed her boat in and, with flashing oars, dared them to come closer.

They did not dare take the challenge. To cut across the path of Sadie's boat at that moment would mean a collision, one which they themselves would precipitate. This, according to Miss Talley's rules, would automatically put them out of the race.

In triumph, Jo and Sadie closed up the distance between them and their rivals. Now they were neck and neck. Now they were a little ahead!

"Hooray for the last stretch!" thought Jo to herself, and her muscles responded joyfully to the task she set them.

Sadie's back bent and unbent rhythmically to the long sweep of the oars. Her lips were set and her eyes blazed with determination.

The girls on shore saw them coming as they rounded the bend of the island. At first it was impossible to tell who was in the lead. One boat stood out from the others, a full half-length ahead.

Whose boat was it?

It was evident that Kate and Lottie thought their friends were in the winning craft.

"It's Ruth and Carol!" cried Kate, tossing her head. "We might have known they'd win."

"Come on, Ruth! Come on, Carol!" cried Lottie.

A few scattered voices took up the cry. But for the most part the girls were silent, intent upon the small fleet of boats as it swept down the lake.

It was evident, even from that distance, that only two of the boats had a chance to win—the one on the inside of the course and that next to it. The other two trailed behind, hopelessly out of the running.

Suddenly Nan started up with a joyful shout.

"That's Jo and Sadie in the leading boat!" she cried. "Hurrah for Sade! Hurrah for Jo! They cut in. They're going to win! They're going to win! They're going to win!!!"

"Don't be so sure of that!" cried Lottie Sparks, her eyes snapping. "The race isn't won yet!"

But her last words were lost in a great shout of excitement.

The two boats were half way between the island and the boathouse now, Sadie and Jo still holding the lead.

But the second boat was creeping up, up, gradually but steadily closing the distance between them.

"Why doesn't Sade increase the stroke?" thought Jo desperately. "It would be awful to let them win after all!"

Up, up, crept the rival boat. Sadie gritted her teeth, but kept to the even, regular stroke.

"Not yet! Not yet!" she said to herself, resisting the impulse to dash madly ahead, outdistancing her rival. "We'll win, but I've got to use my head. If I can hold Jo down, we'll be all right. If she loses the stroke, we're lost!"

Neck and neck now! Carol's boat was nosing out ahead! Only fifty feet from the line represented by Miss Talley's boat! To those on shore it looked as if only one finish were possible. Kate and her cronies were openly triumphant; Nan and her friends still fiercely defiant, but losing hope.

"Come on, Sadie. Come on, Jo!" begged Nan wildly. "You can do it yet! You can beat 'em!"

"Let's see them do it!" cried Lottie Sparks, above the uproar.

"Here they come! Here they come!" Jessie gripped Nan's arm and whirled her around, pointing toward the water. "Sadie! Jo! Hooray!"

The sound of frantic cheering rose and swelled to a roar as Sadie and Jo, in a beautiful burst of speed, overtook their rivals, oars flashing in the sun, outdistanced them, flashed past Miss Talley's boat!

The roar of the little cannon again, reverberating over the still water, echoing from shore to shore.

Victory was theirs! Jo and Sadie had won!

As the second boat flashed across the line the school chant reached the ears of the victors.

"Laurel Hall! Laurel Hall!
Laurel Hall for aye!
Jo and Sadie! Jo and Sadie!
They have won the day!
Jo and Sadie! Jo and Sadie!
Ray! Ray! Ray!"

It was a great day for these two girls of Woodford. They had distinguished themselves on the lake as Nan had distinguished herself on the tennis courts. They felt that Laurel Hall was proud of them and they were supremely happy.

It was only at night as they undressed slowly, still talking over the exciting event of the day, that Nan struck a discordant note.

"Kate and Lottie are more furious with us than ever," she said. "After you had won I saw them go off together, whispering. I saw them look in our direction several times, and I know that they were plotting something. We'll have to watch out for those girls more than ever now!"

About three days after the boat races the girls were again

out on the lake when they met Frank Gibbs, Fred Fielding, and Dodd Martyn, the boys who had figured in their adventure on Huckleberry Island.

The young fellows were vastly excited.

"Our camp has been visited by thieves and practically cleaned out," said Dodd Martyn. "We had to go down to Laurelton and lay in a new stock of five-and-ten-cent store things."

"The funny thing was that they never took anything of value," Fred added. "Most of our belongings were tin— —"

"Except our bathing suits, of course," broke in Frank, with a grin. "But even they were sort of moth-eaten and uninviting. Nothing to tempt a thief, you'd say!"

After they returned to the Hall the girls thought a great deal about this new turn of events.

"Stealing bathing suits and things," Jo repeated dreamily. "Sounds sort of familiar, doesn't it? Like the theft of gym and bathing suits from the gym and the boathouse?"

"You mean it looks as though the same thief robbed both places?" Sadie asked, and Jo nodded.

That was in the afternoon.

About twelve o'clock that same night Nan woke up. She got up to get a drink of water. It was bright moonlight and, chancing to look from the window, Nan's glance fell upon something that instantly chained her attention.

A motor boat was stealing up to the dock!

There was a slight sound behind her, and she started and turned swiftly.

"It's only Jo and me," came Sadie's voice. "We heard you, and thought maybe you were sick. Are you?"

"No. But come here and look at this!"

She pointed from the window to the motor boat, which was clearly visible upon the moonlit water. As the other girls peered curiously over Nan's shoulder, two men jumped up on the dock. One of them disappeared about the corner of the boathouse, the other made hurriedly for the gymnasium.

"The thieves!" cried Jo. "We've seen them at last!"

The three girls hurried out into the corridor to get a better view from a window there than any of their own afforded.

"Wait a minute! Look!" Sadie was shaking with excitement. "That man has come out of the gym and he's heading for the garage! He is opening the door!"

"Miss Jane's sedan! He's stealing Miss Jane's car!" cried Nan. "Come on, girls, quick! We've got to give the alarm!"

But Jo caught her arm.

"Look over there! That light from the gym!" she gasped. "Girls, the gym is on fire!"

CHAPTER XXIV

A DASTARDLY PLOT

In a moment all was excitement, confusion, panic. If Nan and Jo had not acted quickly, probably the gymnasium would have gone up in smoke.

As it was they, with Miss Romaine, a score of teachers, the head janitor and the other men about the place reached it in time to fight the fire with hand grenades and, eventually, conquer it.

Taken at the start, the fire was not allowed to gain much headway. It started in the north end of the gymnasium, insidiously crept along the woodwork, reaching for the heavily beamed ceiling.

Streams of chemicals played hissingly upon the flames, beating them down gradually but relentlessly. A great sigh of thankfulness greeted the defeat of the last feeble, sullen flame.

The janitor picked up a lamp from the debris.

"This is what started it, ma'am," he said, turning to Miss Romaine. "Some one must have been here with this thing lighted and then kicked it over in his hurry to get out."

Miss Romaine glanced at the faces of the girls, some frightened, some merely excited, and she suddenly assumed her air of authority.

"All the danger is over, girls," she said in a tone that did not permit of argument. "Go back to bed and to sleep at once. I will have no further discussion of this unpleasant happening to-night."

So it came about that the girls did not hear of the additional theft of articles from the gymnasium and the boathouse until the following morning.

Also Miss Romaine's sedan was gone. The thieves had left no trace behind them except the broken lamp which had furnished a clue to the cause of the fire in the gymnasium.

The students of Laurel Hall went about with very serious faces all that day.

"This thing is going a little bit too far," they told each other gloomily. "The thieves tried to burn the school down last night. Who knows but what, next time, they may succeed!"

One timid girl even wanted to go home.

Meanwhile, the rivalry between Kate Speed and her followers and the girls from Woodford and their friends became more intense.

Thwarted in every attempt to beat the three girl chums in honest sport, Kate and Lottie resorted to dishonesty and nursed a plot that, if discovered, would forever bar them from Laurel Hall.

These girls knew the danger, but were willing to take the chance of possible discovery and disgrace for the sake of evening the score with their enemies.

So it chanced that while the three chums were in class one day, Lottie Sparks slipped into their room.

She possessed herself of some odd objects—a signet ring of Nan's that she seldom wore, a handkerchief with Jo's name embroidered on it, a letter addressed to Sadie which had been carelessly left on the table by the latter.

Having secreted these things about her person, Lottie smiled to herself and glided from the room.

That night a shadow stole down to Miss Romaine's office. Moonlight streaming in at the window revealed the face and form of Lottie Sparks.

Lottie worked quickly but stealthily. She opened the drawers of Miss Romaine's desk—always a model of neatness—and rummaged the papers about until they were in complete disorder. Some of them she removed and scattered over the floor.

Then she took the articles stolen from the chums' room and placed them about the office so that they would appear to have been dropped by accident and yet could not fail to be discovered.

After this she took an inkwell from one of the drawers of the desk and deliberately turned it upside down in the center of Miss Romaine's beautiful rug!

She overturned a chair, pulled one curtain from the rod, and was about to muss up the place still further when she was arrested by a sudden sound.

In alarm she shrank back into the shadows, her eyes fixed upon a doorway in the far corner of the room.

The door opened, the figure of a man slipped through stealthily and stopped in the position of a crouching animal.

Lottie waited for no more, but with quaking limbs she turned and fled.

Upstairs in her bed she cowered beneath the covers and waited, shivering, for the dawn.

With morning came a terrible revelation for the girls of Laurel Hall.

Miss Romaine's office had been entered during the night. Her papers had been scattered about. Some were lost, others ruined.

But this was by no means the worst. The office safe had been opened. Valuable bonds had been taken, together with some other, practically worthless, non-negotiable securities.

But the mysterious, the staggering thing was the fact that articles belonging to the three girls from Woodford had been found among the scattered papers on the floor—an envelope bearing the name of Sadie Appleby, Nan's signet ring, Jo's handkerchief.

Strong evidence, one would say—and yet there was not a girl in Laurel Hall, outside of Kate Speed's own crowd, who would believe one word against the girls from Woodford!

"There's something more to this than meets the eye," said Jessie Robinson, haranguing a group of students later in the day on the campus. "I'll tell you, girls, it's a frame-up, and I'm willing to bet anything I own that I know who's at the bottom of it, too."

"Just let us get our hands on them, that's all!" cried a chorus of them. Kate Speed and Lottie Sparks, crossing the campus at that moment, were made the target for a score of angry glances.

Kate tossed her head and walked on. But it might have been noticed that Lottie slipped behind her friend, as though she were trying to hide from the sight of her accusing schoolmates.

As a matter of fact, Lottie was in a panic. Terrified at the enormity of the thing she had done—a twist of Fate had turned a girlish prank into a criminal offense, punishable by law. She would have gone at once to Miss Romaine and confessed, but Kate held her back.

"What do you want to do—get us all in trouble?" Kate demanded. "You just sit tight and keep still. Those Woodford girls are going to get what's coming to them! It's about time, too!"

And what of "those Woodford girls?" How were they taking this serious charge against them?

For a time they were more stunned than anything else. The charge was so outrageous that it seemed impossible to take it seriously. Yet they were aware that it was serious enough. They were more than ever aware of this when they received word from Miss Romaine, summoning them to the office.

The summons was brought to them by Lily Darrow. The girl looked as pale and sickly as ever, yet there was unusual determination in her step, in the set of her mouth.

"I'm going with you," she told the girls as they left the room together. "I asked Miss Romaine if I could stay in the office, and she said I could. I may—" She paused, then added in a low voice: "I may have something to tell her."

The girls glanced at her suspiciously. After all, although Lily Darrow had always seemed friendly toward them, she was constantly seen with Kate Speed. Probably her sympathies were with that side. Perhaps she had come, at Kate's bidding, to add further "evidence" to the already staggering amount against them.

They reached Miss Romaine's door. Jo pushed it open and they stepped within the office.

Miss Romaine was at her desk, and as the girls entered she looked up at them gravely. Before her, within reach of her fingers, were a signet ring, a handkerchief and the envelope of a letter.

The girls looked dumbly at these things, then steadily met Miss Romaine's glance as it rested upon each of them in turn.

"Have you girls any idea how these articles came to be in my office on the night of the robbery?" she asked.

Before they could reply in their own defense, Lily Darrow stepped up to the desk. Her eyes blazed black in her white face but her chin was held high as she said, in a startlingly clear voice:

"I can tell you, Miss Jane. I know all about it!"

CHAPTER XXV

THE LOOT RECOVERED

In answer to Miss Romaine's quick, intent questions Lily Darrow told her story.

The girl chums listened, surprised and bewildered at first, but growing more and more excited as they realized the importance to themselves of what this strange girl could reveal.

Lily told of overhearing the plot between Kate and Lottie; a plot the schemers hoped would convict the Woodford girls of the sort of practical joke least likely to be tolerated by Miss Romaine.

"She told Kate about seeing the robber come in that door," said Lily, pointing dramatically. "And how, after mussing the office all up and scattering the girls' things about, she was scared to death and ran up to her room and lay in bed all night with the covers over her head. So you see, Miss Jane, Nan and Jo and Sadie didn't know a thing about it!" Then, having finished her evidence, this unaccountable girl burst into tears and, with her hands to her face, rushed from the room.

The girls looked after her, wondering, then turned to Miss Romaine, who was absently toying with a paper weight on her desk.

"I am glad for your sake, my dear girls, that you have found so good a friend in Lily Darrow," she said slowly. "A girl has indeed proved her friendship who is willing to risk her future for it."

A wondering glance passed between the chums.

"I don't think we quite understand, Miss Jane," said Nan hesitantly.

"No, I don't suppose you would, without knowing more of the circumstances." Miss Romaine seemed to consider; then spoke with quick resolution. "Lily Darrow has not known the happy life that most of you girls have had. Her mother and father died about three years ago, leaving the girl an orphan and penniless. Mr. Speed, Kate's father, took her into his household—I believe she was a distant relation—as a companion to Kate. I imagine she has been more of a servant than a companion."

Here the girls exchanged glances that said they could easily believe that, too.

"At any rate," added Miss Romaine, still toying with the paper weight, "if I expel Kate and Lottie—as they richly deserve—Lily would have to go with them. Kate would see to that."

Jo made a quick sound of pity.

"I know now what you meant about Lily's sacrifice for friendship!" she said.

Miss Romaine nodded, studying the girls.

"It would be a double pity to separate Lily from Laurel Hall since her entire future—and a pleasant one, I think—depends upon her connection here." Taking pity on the girls' bewilderment, she added, looking steadily at them, "I have taken a great interest in Lily Darrow. She is a good student. In all her classes she stands at or near the head. I have promised her a position on my staff of teachers as soon as she has finished here. I think," she added slowly, "that Lily Darrow is living for that."

"And she would sacrifice everything for us," said Sadie, wondering. Then she added quickly: "Oh, Miss Romaine, isn't there something we can do? There must be something!"

"Yes, there is something," said Miss Romaine slowly. "It all depends on whether you girls will agree."

She went on to say that if Lottie and Kate were severely punished but not expelled, if the name of the girl who overheard their plot could be kept out of the matter entirely, Lily Darrow might yet escape the penalty of her brave act.

"If I can have the coöperation of you girls," said Miss Romaine, with her grave smile, "I think I can manage everything satisfactorily. We will be partners in a kindly conspiracy that will do no harm to any one and may do some one a great deal of good."

The girls agreed eagerly, glad to have mercy upon Kate and Lottie if by so doing they could benefit the poor girl whose odd association with Kate Speed was now made clear to them.

But there were still the mysterious robberies at the school to be explained. The morale of the students was seriously affected by the repeated alarms. They were nervous and jumpy, predicting direful mishaps in the near future, and several went over to the side of the timid girl who wanted to go home.

Miss Romaine, desperate at the inertia of the local police, was talking of hiring city detectives.

Things were at this pass when Nan met Frank Gibbs one day and the young fellow asked her to make up a party for one last outing on the lake. The boys had already met Miss Romaine, and she rather encouraged the friendship between them and the three girl chums.

"Isn't it pretty cold?" protested Nan, who, with the other girls, had resorted to sweaters and sport coats. "We are apt to freeze to death."

"Not if we make the kind of fire I'm thinking about," the boy retorted, with a grin. "Come on, be a good sport. We'll roast potatoes and have a real party."

When Nan passed thc invitation on to Sadie and Jo they assented more readily than she had expected.

"We need something to take our minds off robbers and mysteries and things," Sadie added. "I've reached the point where every little shadow holds a villain all its own."

"And I've found out I have nerves," Jo added gloomily. "That's an entirely new discovery for me. Sure! Let's go and roast potatoes. It will do us good."

So, having received permission from Miss Romaine, they set off the following Saturday for Buttercup Island, which was some distance down the lake. The boys had chosen this particular island because on it was plenty of the kind of wood they would need for building a campfire.

Buttercup Island was visited little by the girls from Laurel Hall, since it was neither as accessible nor as pretty as some nearer the school.

When they arrived the boys already had a splendid fire going. In it potatoes and eggs were rolled indiscriminately, and the cooks were getting ready a huge pile of frankfurters for roasting.

"Every one's got to cook his own," said Dodd Martyn, pointing to some long, sharp-pointed twigs prepared for the purpose.

"No work—no eat, that's the rule in this camp," added Fred Fielding.

The girls were glad enough to work, for there was a chill wind blowing from the water, a keen-edged wind that made any sort of work agreeable.

"We'll soon have to be going home," said Frank regretfully, as they gathered about the fire some time later, to eat blackened potatoes, blackened frankfurters, and eggs cooked far too hard for good taste or good digestion. "It's apt to snow in a few days, and snow sure takes the fun out of camping."

"I should think it would." Nan paused with a frankfurter half way to her lips and stared off through the trees. "There's a motor boat," she said as they all turned to follow her gaze.

"With two men in it," added Sadie.

"And it's making straight for this island!" cried Jo. She was on her feet in an instant, staring at the incoming motor boat.

Nan pulled her down to the ground again.

"Don't let them see you," she cried. "If they land we can get a really good look at them."

All watched with intense interest as the motor boat neared the island, rounded a small promontory, and put in to shore. There was something familiar about the motor boat and about the men in it, too!

"If it should be Andrew Simmer!" thought Jo, a wild hope in

her heart. To Fred Fielding she whispered urgently: "Don't let them get away. If they see us and start to run, catch them. Promise me!"

Fred nodded.

"Don't talk!" he said. "Here they come!"

The two men came slowly up the bank. One of them carried a pack on his back and looked like a tramp. The other was—Jo got a good look at his face this time and choked back a cry—Andrew Simmer!

The men saw neither the fire nor the young people about it, but kept on along the shores of the lake toward some definite objective.

Their hearts beating fast, the girls and boys followed.

The two men, looking neither to the right nor to the left of them, shuffled doggedly along. After a few moments they struck off into the deepest part of the woods, the young folks still trailing at a cautious distance.

"One of those rascals robbed our camp," Frank whispered to Nan. "I caught a glimpse of him that same day, hanging about in the woods— —"

"Sh!" said Nan, finger to lips. "Look, they have disappeared!"

Running eagerly forward, the young people found that the hole through which the men had disappeared was the mouth of a cave. Jo's eyes were shining with a wild hope.

"We'll wait here till they come out again," she said to Fred.

"And then we'll nab 'em!" Fred finished with a nod. "Watch us!"

The two rascals reappeared so quickly that the boys were almost taken off their guard. Almost—but not quite.

As the men emerged from the cave, blinking in the strong light, the three boys fell upon them with all the vigor of youth and an earnest desire for revenge.

Andrew Simmer started to put up a fight, but when he saw Jo's angry face and blazing eyes, her little fists raised as though to add their weight to the battle, he crumpled and began to babble incoherently.

"I didn't do it—I didn't!" he said, fairly groveling at Jo's feet while Fred stood back and watched him with astonishment. "Tell your father I didn't do it! I It's all a mistake! Don't let them put me in prison! Don't!"

Frank Gibbs and Dodd Martyn had overpowered the tramp. Dodd was now sitting upon the latter's chest, regarding the scene with great interest.

Jo took a step closer to Andrew Simmer. All her wrongs and her father's surged over her, filling her with fury.

"You are a cowardly scoundrel, Andrew Simmer!" she cried, flaying the wretched fellow mercilessly. "You have wrecked my father's business. You have broken his heart and threatened his very life. You deserve to be hung!"

"Oh, no, spare me, spare me!" cried Simmer, in an agony of fear. "I will make restitution. I will do anything! Only spare my life!"

The prostrate tramp wriggled and tried to get up—whereupon Frank Gibbs joined Dodd Martyn on his chest. The tramp subsided, muttering imprecations.

"Then where," cried Jo, her voice thick with mingled hope and fear, "are my father's papers?"

For a tense second Andrew Simmer hesitated. Then he raised himself and pointed dramatically to the cave.

"In there!" he said. "You will find everything in there!"

The girls brought ropes from the launch and the boys bound their captives fast. Then, together, they thoroughly searched the cave.

Articles stolen from the gymnasium and the boathouse at Laurel Hall were brought to light, proving the identity of the robbers. Sadie found a packet of papers, evidently the loot from Miss Romaine's office desk.

But it was Nan who brought forth a black box marked with Mr. Morley's name.

"Look here, Jo," she said in an odd tone. "I believe this belongs to you!"

Jo gave one look at the box and its contents, then sat down very quietly with it in her lap and began to cry.

Nan and Sadie ran to her in swift sympathy, while the boys looked awkwardly on.

"Don't cry, honey," they coaxed, arms about her. "Don't cry!"

"I—I can't help it! I'm so—so happy." Jo lifted to them a face on which a joyful smile was dawning. "Anyway," she said stoutly, "I'm n-not crying—I'm laughing!"

So it all turned out beautifully after all.

Andrew Simmer and the other man captured by the girls and the boys on the island were hailed into court and there the mystery of their companionship was solved.

The suspicion that Andrew Simmer was not in his right mind when he decamped from Woodford with some vitally important and negotiable papers from his employer's safe in his possession appeared to be well founded.

The tramp, a rough, sly fellow, had come across Simmer just at the time when the latter was in the most acute terror lest his crime be detected. In some way the tramp had succeeded in wresting a confession from the wretched man and had afterward held this over his head as a club, forcing him to commit further robberies in the hope that the first might go undetected.

The black box contained practically all of Mr. Morley's missing papers intact and these, returned to him, put his business once more on a firm foundation.

When the question was raised by Jo as to why the bonds, some of them practically as negotiable as banknotes, had not been turned into cash, Mr. Morley himself replied by letter that both Simmer and the tramp had probably the common sense to hold the bonds until the hue and cry over the robbery had subsided and it was not quite so dangerous to put them in the market.

Among other things found in the cave were a number of pawn tickets. These, redeemed, returned to the girls practically all the articles taken from the boathouse and the gymnasium.

Even the sedan stolen on the night of the fire was recovered in due course of time and returned to its owner. All was well. The world once more became a sensible, well-ordered place and Laurel Hall settled down into its usual routine.

One day, not long after the capture of the thieves, Nan flung into the room where Sadie and Jo were hard at work over lessons. Nan's face was rosy, for she had been walking in a rather keen wind—a wind that prophesied the imminence of winter and of white clad hills.

"Hail and hello!" she greeted them, as the girls looked up absently from their books. "Lend me your ears, friends. I bring you news."

"And you do well," returned Jo, grinning. "That is, if it's good," she qualified. "If it be bad, out, out upon you, wretch, and leave us to our meditations!"

"It's both," returned Nan, flinging her hat on the bed. "Speedy Kate and Lottie have been denied all recreation periods for the next month."

"Miss Jane's punishment," said Sadie, and added: "How did you find out?"

"Lily told me," Nan replied. "She's the gratefulest girl you ever saw—though I keep telling her we are the girls who ought to be grateful. I have more news, too," she added. "The boys are breaking camp. It's getting a little too breezy, even for them. They are going home to-morrow."

"I wonder if we'll ever see them again," said Sadie regretfully.

Jo chuckled.

"I've rather a notion that we shall!" she said.

Jo was right. The friendship between the boys and girls, so oddly begun, ripened with the years into something stronger. Older heads in Woodford began to nod meaningly and matchmaking tongues wagged busily with an old, yet ever new and entrancing subject.

The scene shifts to the pleasant garden at the rear of the Harrison house several years after the opening of this story.

Nan's Aunt Emma, an invalid no longer but a handsome,

happy woman in full possession of her health and joy in life, was seated on the garden bench, smiling over a great pile of letters that lay in her lap.

The sound of laughing voices caused her to look up as Jo and Sadie—older now, "practically grown up"—came swinging down the path toward her, arms entwined.

"What a pretty picture," laughed Jo. "Dreaming over a pack of old letters! Why, Aunt Emma—" as her eyes rested on the writing—"those are my letters to you!"

Miss Emma smiled.

"Your journal dear. I brought them out here to read them again—and remember how much I owe the author of them!"

"Foolish!" said Jo affectionately as she rubbed her fresh cheek against the older one. "How many times do I have to tell you that a good turn always deserves another! Think what you did for me! We saw Nan and Frank just now," she added, with a twinkle in her eyes.

"Oh, didn't we just!" agreed Sadie. "You'd never guess what they were doing, Aunt Emma!"

"What were they doing?" asked Miss Emma, an arm about each of the girls.

"They were walking along Main Street, looking in furniture stores," giggled Jo. "They were so absorbed they didn't even see us!"

"At that, Nan might do worse," remarked Sadie enigmatically. "Frank's an awfully nice boy."

"So is Fred Fielding," remarked Miss Emma, playfully pinching Sadie's cheek. "And," turning to Jo, "I've never remarked anything particularly wrong with Dodd Martyn, either!"

Across Miss Emma, Jo's eyes and Sadie's met. They smiled.

"Yes," sighed Sadie, "they are both nice boys."

Jo nodded profoundly.

"They are both awfully nice boys!" she said. "Especially Dodd!"

"Especially Fred!" said Sadie.

www.ingramcontent.com/pod-product-compliance
Ingram Content Group UK Ltd.
Pitfield, Milton Keynes, MK11 3LW, UK
UKHW012249290726
14090UKWH00013B/545